Mischief in Moonstone Series, Novella 2: Misbehavin' in Moonstone

By Christine DeSmet

Writers Exchange E-Publishing
http://www.writers-exchange.com

Mischief in Moonstone Series, Novella 2: Misbehavin' in Moonstone
Copyright 2017, 2023, 2025 Christine DeSmet
Writers Exchange E-Publishing
PO Box 372
ATHERTON QLD 4883

Cover Art by: Sandy Cummins

Published by Writers Exchange E-Publishing
http://www.writers-exchange.com

Chapter 1

"The men are missing." Kirsten Peplinski stood in her white chef's hat and apron staring at an empty restaurant on a Friday night. On a hot July evening, the place should've been filled with locals lapping up her bluegill special. "Don't look at me that way, Crystal. Three afternoons and nights in a row--no men in Moonstone. No money in my register."

With a cockeyed smile, Crystal Hagan, a redhead almost twenty years older than fair-haired Kirsten, clutched a stack of bridal magazines. "Kirstie, nobody's been able to pass on your garlic mashed potatoes since you opened *The Jingle Bell Inn* last month. I heard they're only fishing." But Kirsten had a bad feeling. She popped off her hat to run fingers through chin-length hair. "This much fishing? Is there a tournament?"

"Not that I know of, but you know how men can be."

"Unfortunately. That's why I prefer being busy."

Crystal laughed, settling in with her magazines at a maple table that normally held four paying customers by five o'clock. "Maybe you should go fishing. If Peter were back from Phoenix that's where I'd be. Since moving back to Wisconsin the man has become addicted to fishing. Recapturing a missed childhood."

Kirsten scrunched her starched hat. "They're boycotting my restaurant, aren't they? Because of..." She swallowed the secret that Crystal and only a precious few others knew. Kirsten had been born in Moonstone, but some unfortunate events during her teenage years had sent her packing. "What've they been saying about me around Moonstone?"

"I can't decide between sleeveless or cap sleeves. Do you think I'm too old for sleeveless?"

Groaning, Kirsten plopped down at the table. Ever since Crystal Hagan and Peter LeBarron had decided on a wedding date, all Kirsten could get out of her friend were lopsided grins, twinkles in her green eyes, and more effervescence than the Italian sodas Kirsten served.

"You're sure it's not about what happened back then?" She hadn't wanted to return to the village on the shores of Lake Superior, but her mother had insisted, threatening to have another heart attack. Thus, all three of the Peplinski women had returned to Moonstone, ring-leader Grandma included. Crystal ripped out a page picturing a veil. "Do you think a princess crown with the veil would be too pretentious?"

"You'll be a princess to your first-graders. Go for the crown."

"A crown it is."

Kirsten wished she could be that worry-free. The Jingle Bell Inn was located in what used to be the lavish dining hall of the historic mansion called the North Pole, a place replete with green roof, red trim, and creamy white siding. It got its name because the elderly owner and upstairs resident, Henri LeBarron, had played Santa Claus for the town's Christmas celebrations for years. Henri was Peter's father. They'd given Kirsten a second chance at "doing good" in life. She didn't mind philanthropy. But now she'd fallen in love with the place. Its possibilities let her have dreams for the first time in her life.

The outdoor setting was as magical as the interior's polished oak floors with their inlaid designs. A sweeping yard hugged the craggy, Lake Superior shoreline. Tall pines and white birch rimmed the property. If the restaurant succeeded, she wanted to add a deck and patio for music and special events. But now that dream looked elusive. She was about to go out of business.

But because of fishing?

"Maybe my prices are too high."

Tisking at her, Crystal ripped out two more pages. "The trout are active on the Brule River, what with the mosquito hatch we've had."

It had to be something more. Kirsten's pride couldn't accept being beat by biting bugs. "Should I offer entertainment? I could clear the far corner for dancing."

"Don't even go there with your background."

Heat shimmied up Kirsten's neck and face. "You're right."

Somehow she had to win back the men. At twenty-five and fresh out of college, she was expected to fail. Refusing to succumb, she shot off the chair. "Can you watch things for me?" As if there was anything to watch.

"Where're you going?"

"I haven't a clue. To find the men and bring them back here."

Crystal held up a page again, green eyes going dewy. She wasn't going to be any help.

Kirsten swallowed her distress. "Wouldn't the sleeveless version be cold for a Christmas wedding?"

Crystal swooned. "Peter suggested taking advantage of the flower gardens out back that I've been restoring. Could you handle cooking for two hundred guests, say in a couple of weeks?"

Kirsten flinched. "Say what?"

"Okay, a month?"

Since Crystal would technically be her boss by marriage--soon, it appeared--Kirsten nodded, swallowing a whimper.

She hurried out and down the mansion's broad sidewalk. With hot sun slanting from the west, fighting through thick humidity, she almost ran headlong into the mayor's wife. Even the limpest hair stood up on the nape of Kirsten's neck.

Built like a bulldog never been denied a treat in its life, silver-haired Tootsie Winters blocked the sidewalk, panting. She'd stuffed herself into a red, flower-spangled sleeveless blouse and matching capris. "Good grief but it's hot. I heard eighty-five. Can you believe that? Right here next to the lake?"

Kirsten considered bolting. "Yeah, it's mighty hot, Mrs. Winters."

"What's on special? Bob already eating my share?"

"I think he's fishing."

Tootsie's jowls shook. "Again? He's been fishing for three days now."

"They've all been fishing. Haven't you noticed? And look there."

The town was so small they could see from one end of the main drag to the other. Cars glided by. Kirsten was tempted to lie down in the street in an attempt to get customers. "Nobody's stopped in the past three days."

"Damn fishing," Tootsie mused. "It's a religion here, just like Friday night fish fries. Did you change a recipe? I told Bob you were too young to handle this."

Too young? That was her concern? Not the rap sheet? But Tootsie was concerned about money. The five-person Chamber of Commerce had given a grant to Kirsten to help her buy restaurant equipment and start up Moonstone's first new business in years. Tootsie had argued that grants should go to people who had far more experience than a "college student cooking snooty food in a funny hat". Kirsten reminded her that a chef's hat was called a "toque". Tootsie hadn't liked it that her husband had voted for the "toque grant".

"I knew this would happen," Tootsie said. "People around here expect a cook to be professional looking."

Kirsten chewed on a lip to keep from talking. She had a tendency to say all the wrong things.

Tootsie prattled on. "Maybe you should put a perm in your straight hair, wear mascara. You can't really tell that you have eyelashes. Maybe you're freaking people out."

Her fingers coiled into fists, but Kirsten forced herself to relax. "I'll try mascara. Thanks for the tip, Mrs. Winters. Is there anything going on in Duluth at the harbor? A fair? Maybe there's a beer tent?"

"Not that I know of. Bob prefers brandy over beer. He hates loud music. That's why he likes your place. It's always dead."

Kirsten choked that down as a compliment. "Excuse me, but I've got to find out why my regulars aren't here."

"I'll come with. It's not like Bob to miss a meal." The older woman strutted her heft down the sidewalk ahead of Kirsten, taking command like the Pied Piper of Moonstone. "Rita might know what's going on."

Rita Johnson ran the post office which sat on a rocky lot west of the LeBarron mansion. Rita wasn't there, so they headed across the town's open square to the bar. All they found was a sign on the locked door: "Gone fishing. Back at ten p.m. Lucas."

Tootsie looked as perplexed as Kirsten. "Lucas is always open on Fridays. He has that special on brandy old-fashioneds. Bob and I were coming here after dinner at your place. That's another thing you need. A bar."

Got it. Mascara and a bar. How about customers?

There was one more possibility--the hardware store on the corner, run by Rita Johnson's husband, Greg. He sold live bait and fishing equipment. The lack of cars parked on the streets gave Kirsten little hope.

The place smelled of rope and twine, oil paint, and stale coffee, but no men. Kirsten would give anything to whiff a little cigar smoke, fish guts, and sweat.

Rita was alone at the counter putting orange sales tags on clear plastic bags of rubber worms. "Greg didn't say where he was going. He called as I was locking up the post office and asked if I could fill in. I assume he's picking up supplies in Duluth. We're out of bug spray."

Tootsie puffed, "Out of bug spray?! You can't expect us all to wear long sleeves and pants in this weather. Those damn mosquitoes are killing me."

"Toots, if you wouldn't wear that dime store perfume you'd attract fewer mosquitoes and keep your husband close to you instead."

Kirsten turned away so Tootsie wouldn't see her smirk.

Tootsie ran a hand across her sweaty forehead. "I'm not the problem. It seems the men have up and gone fishing again."

"It's what we want them to do in summer," mused Rita, writing new prices on the tags.

Tootsie persisted, to Kirsten's surprise. "They haven't shown up for Kirstie's garlic mashed potatoes. As much as this pains me to say, they are pretty darn good. They don't even require gravy."

Rita put down the worms. "You know, this *is* odd. Every Friday night we go out for fish. They're fishing? Again?"

Kirsten nodded. "Henri was sitting out in his chair watching traffic and told me a guy waved from a truck and invited him to come along. Something about fishing being the new Viagra."

"Viagra?" yelped Tootsie. "Bob's heart can't handle that stuff."

Rita grunted. "You know, three fishing days in a row is a bit much. Greg wouldn't miss your pan-seared bluegills with the garlic mashed potatoes and cheddar cheesy muffins."

"With the blueberry pie and Kirsten's homemade vanilla ice cream."

Kirsten beamed in shock. "Thank you, Mrs. Winters. You sound as if you're on my side."

Tootsie squared her shoulders. "Having a restaurant here beats driving into Duluth. It's all about saving gas money."

"Of course." Kirsten wanted to mutter something about Tootsie not needing any more gas, but instead said to Rita, "Maybe Greg knows what's going on? Somebody must have stopped by today and said something."

"Good thought." Rita punched a button on her cell phone, then frowned. "That's odd. He must've turned his phone off. He never does that." Rita stared at the phone as if her husband would pop out.

Tootsie called her husband. She, too, got no answer. "Now I am concerned. Bob needs his food and pills on time to keep his blood pressure in check."

Kirsten offered, "Fishing's supposed to be relaxing."

"Bob doesn't need to relax. That's his problem," said Tootsie. "If he'd do more around the house, he'd lose weight. Did you know vacuuming is worth about three hundred steps toward your ten-thousand a day? What's fishing? Ten steps to find a place to plop the beer cooler so you can sit and watch your bobber on the water."

Kirsten was saved from responding by the door flapping open.

Three frowning women sashayed in amid a whoosh of hot, humid air. Though Kirsten had seen them before in her restaurant, she didn't know their names. Tootsie introduced Jeri Kaminski, with long, blonde hair that Kirsten admired. The woman drove a bus when school was in session and had the muscular arms to go with the job. The petite, freckled brunette, Lily Bauer, wearing a string of pearls, was the head teller at the bank. Both maybe in their thirties, they wore conservative sundresses, too much makeup, and carried handbags that matched their dresses and sandals. The fiftyish, plump but curvaceous, dark-haired Margie Mueller wore a pink blouse with buttons bursting and matching pink pants. She managed the IGA grocery. Maybe looking like a giant strawberry was appropriate for a grocer. Kirsten hadn't socialized enough in Moonstone to know the fashion rules.

Jeri declared, "I thought our guys would be here. They were supposed to meet us at The Jingle Bell Inn. Don't tell me they're fishing again."

The comely Lily fingered her pearls. "We truly must stop this fishing thing. Three days without my man makes me itch."

Margie sniffled, fanning her generous cleavage. "Some blind date this has been so far. This is the last time I let you two do this to me. I even bought a new bra just in case."

In case of--? Kirsten didn't want to ask. "Maybe the guys are taking your blind date for a drink first before he meets you."

"He has to drink to get his courage to meet me?" Margie burst into tears, her bosom bouncing despite the new bra.

Kirsten wanted to evaporate. "I'm sorry. I didn't mean it the way it sounded."

Little Lily stretched to pat Margie's ample shoulders. "Please don't cry. Think of your makeup."

Margie bawled louder. The women glared at Kirsten. In a panic she said, "All of you go over to the restaurant for a free dinner. Salad bar's ready. I'll get to the bottom of this and be back in a jiffy."

The women only stood there.

Kirsten's heart fell into her belly. "What's wrong? It's free food."

Jeri frowned. "You want us to go out on Friday night without our men? Kirk and I have been going out for fish on Friday nights together for years. We have our routine. Breaking it means our marriage is breaking."

Lily nodded. "Tom likes to eat early, then we do the hoochy-coo and go to bed by nine."

Did she wear her pearls for that, too?

Rita snapped her fingers. "Greg mentioned how the fishing had been picking up out on the lake. If there's a stiff wind, you know how easy it is to drift east to the casino in Port Cliff."

"Gambling?" Tootsie growled. "When I get my hands on him--"

Margie sucked back a sob. "I suppose I could meet my blind date at the casino for dinner instead of here."

"Ladies," Kirsten blurted, her brain racing. She couldn't lose them to a casino buffet, even though she'd heard good things about the woman who cooked there. "Go over to the Inn. Margie, I'll find your blind date. You're going to fall in love over my bluegills and garlic mashed potatoes. I guarantee it."

"I am?" Margie dabbed a tissue around her eyes.

"Fix your mascara and get ready to bat those eyelashes. You have lovely eyelashes."

"I do?"

Kirsten rushed out. She trotted back to the North Pole to get her car, then drove east out of Moonstone. Traffic was unusually heavy, which worried her. Maybe the casino's food was doing her in. She had driven only a couple of miles along the Lake Superior shoreline, though, before she discovered what had happened to Moonstone's men.

She slammed on the brakes.

Had she just seen...what she thought she saw?

She did a U-turn and pulled into a scenic lookout on a bluff overlooking the lake.

She grabbed her binoculars, got out, then paled at what she saw.

Was that legal?

Chapter 2

"They were topless?!"

"My husband had what on his lap?"

"How many women were there on that boat?"

"A lot of good it did me to buy this new bra."

Rita, Lily, Jeri, and Margie stared back at her from their salads. All Kirsten could do was peep back, "It's true. A floating flotilla of floozies."

The women hit their speed dial buttons to inform all their other women friends about this outrageous development.

Fifteen minutes later, after trips to the restroom, a caravan of twenty cars driven by fuming women snaked out of Moonstone to the lookout point. Kirsten drove alone in the lead, her fingers perspiring on the steering wheel, already sure--however illogical it was--that Tootsie Winters would blame the debauchery on her.

The women, dressed up for Friday night with their missing men, stood in a row in the hot evening breeze, leaning against the railing with binoculars at their eyes.

"Gone fishing for trout? Hah!" Tootsie spat. "By golly his trouser trout is gonna be tied in a knot."

Jeri lowered her binoculars. "I have to drive brats around in a bus to make ends meet and my husband's spending our hard-earned dollars on her?"

"Her" was any number of topless waitresses serving drinks and food on a lengthy, double-decker touring yacht with a slogan painted on its side: "Fishing Should Be Fun".

When Lily gasped that she'd spotted Margie's date, Margie bawled.

"Shhh," said Jeri, "they'll hear us."

Tootsie scoffed, "They've lost their hearing. The only sense they have is in their pants and it's not pointed at us. Their navigational equipment has succumbed to a magnetic field the likes of which we've never seen in these parts."

Kirsten's face warmed at Tootsie's assessment.

Rita's face was red, too, but with anger. "I can't believe Greg lied to me. He actually said he was going to buy rubber worms. Rubbers are more like it."

"I'm killing my husband," snapped out a woman down the line.

Another woman growled, "Too kind. I'm tying mine to a tree, then pouring honey on him. Let him whisper sweet nothings to the bears that cozy up to him."

For the next few days Kirsten witnessed marriages beginning to unravel. On Sunday at lunchtime, usually a busy time for her restaurant, women came in solo. Some men wandered in, but their wives and girlfriends wouldn't even look at them, except for the "I'll kill him" woman who tossed a bowl of Kirsten's cold raspberry soup over her husband's head.

The favorite restaurant of the men now had become the refuge for the women. The problem was the women didn't order much because their appetites were gone. Even Tootsie stuck with the cheap salad bar. Nobody ordered the fancy trout dinners, that was for sure. The phrase "trouser trout" still hung in the air.

Things got worse that next week. Whoever ran the topless fishing boat knew how to publicize it. Moonstone grew over-run with packs of testosterone trouble who drove from miles around to "fish". At first Kirsten hoped for an influx of new customers.

"But, duh." She moaned across the table at Crystal one morning while needlessly polishing silverware in the empty restaurant. "They eat and drink their fill on that boat. The only person getting business is Lucas over at his bar. And that's because he sells those illegal Cuban cigars."

Even Crystal's exuberance had been curbed by the new Moonstone. She tapped her fingers on the table top, not a bridal magazine in sight. "I have to postpone my wedding."

Kirsten put the silverware down. "You can't. I'll be ready. After all, I've got nothing to do now."

"But look what's going on. Henri complained that last night he couldn't sleep for all the trucks tearing through town at midnight with guys tossing firecrackers in the street out front. It's like the O.K. Corral out there. I can't hold a wedding with that going on."

Kirsten sank back in her chair. "I even begged Mrs. Winters to ask Bob about the legalities of the business. That damn boat is beyond our jurisdiction. We can't even get the new governor to stop it."

"He's probably fishing, too."

By that following weekend, Moonstone's streets grew more clogged with pickup trucks and men whooping it up as they traveled between Superior-Duluth and Port Cliff, where the topless fishing tour boat docked. Even limousines with their mysterious blacked-out windows slid through town without stopping.

When Moonstone's story made the Superior paper with the headline, "Mooning Moonstone", Mayor Bob Winters suffered a heart attack. It happened on a Friday morning in mid-July, two weeks after Kirsten's discovery of the topless fishing tour boat.

Filled with wrath, Tootsie Winters returned from the Duluth hospital to call a meeting of the town's women, prevailing on Kirsten to host it that evening. "You've got the space, since you're practically out of business anyway."

Kirsten wanted to be upset, but Tootsie was right.

Tootsie took her place at the hostess station, using it as a lectern. "All in favor of Kirsten becoming mayor, say aye."

"What?! Wait a minute." Kirsten popped up from the back of the room, caught a foot on a table leg and promptly fell on the floor. The "kill my husband" woman helped Kirsten up.

Tootsie said, "We need an interim mayor."

Lily fingered her pearls. "We need somebody neutral to negotiate with the boat owner."

Tootsie added, "The only thing any of us would do is kill the boat owner and dump his body overboard. He's ruining our marriages and relationships. None of us wants to end up in jail for murder. But you're single and have nothing to lose. We're sending you in."

"Sending me in?" Kirsten peeped. So this was how Tootsie was going to get back at her for her husband voting for the toque grant. "I'm your weapon?" Her legs went wobbly. "I'm, I'm not a good talker. I like to hide in the kitchen. It's why I'm a cook. Really."

Rita shrugged. "From what we've seen on the boat, talking's not necessary."

"You're blonde and you don't have wrinkles," Tootsie said. "Put a little makeup on and they'll think you're one of the tarts. You can sneak on, scope it out, get the goods on the man."

Kirsten got to the hostess stand without tripping again. "Ladies, I can't talk to some businessman about his nude women. I mean, ick."

Tootsie huffed, "May I remind you that this town loaned you a bundle of cash?"

Lily, the bank teller, waved her hand. "From our bank. You owe us."

Margie stood up, wringing a hankie in her hand. "I had a chance with this guy. Lily found him on the Internet. All of our interests matched up. Then, poof, I didn't even get to meet the guy. His girlfriend is now some floozy--" She snorted back tears. "Nobody shops at my IGA anymore. Nobody but women, and no offense, but the only things you gals buy are fat free milk and tampons. I can't stay in business much longer."

Several women got up to console Margie.

Kirsten's mouth went dry. "But I'm a nobody. You said it."

"Precisely why you're perfect to lead the charge," Tootsie said. "If you lose and have to leave town, nothing's lost here."

Tootsie was getting on her nerves, but, damn, the woman was right again. Kirsten wanted to cry along with Margie.

Jeri, the bus driver, shot up from her chair. "Honey, you don't even date. You won't be affected by getting on the boat. The rest of us would only blubber at the ogre running the tart ship. We need you because you don't have emotions like we do."

Hmm, these women fought dirty. To them, she was the most pitiful, harmless virgin to toss into the volcano--er, lake--to appease the gods.

The urge to walk out overwhelmed her, but then something in their eyes bolted her to the floor. Could they possibly need her? She was being used because she was lonely and alone. But as pitiful as that sounded, their needing her to lead them felt new, strange--and powerful. She'd never been a boss; she'd always been bossed around, from the time she was a little girl.

"Okay. I'll talk to the owner about his tart ship."

The restaurant erupted into such clapping that Kirsten stepped back from the force of it. While the women smiled at her--some hopping up and down and waving tissues--fear rolled through Kirsten, tasting like cold copper inside her mouth. What had she just done to herself?

That night in her empty restaurant where she'd have privacy, she got on the phone. Her hands shook.

After several tries she connected with a Captain Ricardo. With his thick accent, he was tough to understand, but he agreed to meet tomorrow night after his last run docked at eleven o'clock.

While she dressed in a power suit of navy pants, white camp shirt and a navy jacket despite the warm night, her mother, Ellen, and Grandma Tracy warned her not to go through with this foolishness. The women were echoes of each other. Kirsten had always been struck by the similarities in the Peplinski women. Except for a few more lines in their faces, the older two-- forty-two and fifty-eight, respectively--could pass for Kirsten's sisters with their trim, youthful builds, creamy skin and the famous, white-blonde hair. Unlike Kirsten, they wore their hair long, her mother's locks held back with a headband, her grandmother's captured in a long braid.

Grandma Tracy busied herself by rearranging Kirsten's closet. "Make sure the nudie girls are gone. If you're caught with them, you know we all go to jail. Nude routines got us in trouble last time." She kissed Kirsten on the cheek.

Kirsten's heart lurched. "We're not going to jail. I promise."

Her mother sat on Kirsten's bed, muttering, "The judge told us adamantly to lay low, to get real jobs and to stay out of the headlines. Now you're the mayor."

"Interim mayor. Temporary. In backwoods Wisconsin. It's safe."

Grandma Tracy clapped. "Oh, Ellen, take a moment to enjoy this. To think, my granddaughter a mayor. We really can start over."

But Kirsten's mother blubbered about how she'd been married in a dark suit. "It's a bad omen for you to dress in a dark suit to meet this man."

Kirsten's father had left them when she was a little girl. Her mother always thought it had to do with the bad luck associated with wearing a dark suit instead of a white dress to get married in.

Sitting down next to her mother, Kirsten hugged her. "Now listen, Mom, I'm not marrying the man. I'm only telling him where to shove his boat. Grandma gave me things to say."

"What's your plan?" her mom asked of Grandma Tracy.

"Our plan? With men, it's sex or money," said Grandma Tracy.

Kirsten flinched. "Grandma!"

"Kirstie's all business tonight. She's going to propose something wonderful to the man."

Ellen groaned. "I have the heebie-jeebies." She rose from the bed. "Just make sure this isn't a trap and the sheriff's not lurking with handcuffs."

Kirsten assured her, "We're not wearing that cheap jewelry ever again. Besides, I'm not dressed like I work on the boat. Who would want to arrest me?"

Grandma Tracy flashed a pointed look. "Honey, you're a pretty girl. Make sure he doesn't somehow get you out of those clothes."

After the late night talk show started, Kirsten left their small house hidden on the neglected south side of Moonstone, got in her compact car, then headed through town and hung a right. She passed the dark North Pole mansion then sped along the ribbon of blacktop that cut through tall forest. Flicking on the high beams, she kept careful watch for deer.

About ten minutes later she passed the well-lit Port Cliff casino, then parked at the quiet dock. She took a deep breath. Her armpits were damp. The only lights came from the stars blinking overhead and a single lantern hanging at the end of the pier where the yacht sat.

She eased out of the car. Her heartbeat racing, she looked around, squinting into the shadows. Water slapped against the dock. A wolf howled from far off in the wilderness. Her shoes echoing on the wood planks of the pier, she noticed the air smelled of pines and gasoline from the dock's fuel pump nearby.

She approached the offensive boat, calling, "Hello? Mr. Ricardo?"

Light filtered through a curtain over a window above her. Her armpits dampened more. She'd bet the interior would be all in red, with dim lighting, free cigars smelling up the place, maybe even a pole for special dances, and beds at the ready with mirrors on the ceiling. Shuddering, she shook back memories.

Kirsten saw no cops, no strange men lurking behind trees.

Flapping her jacket to get air to her pits, she called again, "Hello? Captain Ricardo? It's Kirsten Peplinski. The...interim mayor. Interim, okay? Here just to talk."

A squeaking door drew her attention to the bow. A man in a white tuxedo jacket and dark bowtie popped up over the railing.

"Finally, Miss Kirsten Peplinski, we meet. In this light, did you know your hair looks like a halo?"

Kirsten almost peed her pants. He was tall as the moon, which rested on one of his broad shoulders, backlighting wavy, straw-colored hair with a severe side part. She couldn't tell the color of his eyes in the shadows, but their intensity in a craggy face held her fast, as if she'd just met up with the timber wolf she'd heard howling earlier.

"Do your friends call you Kirstie? Or Peppy?"

She stepped back, catching the heel of a pump between the boards. Before toppling and making a fool of herself, she stepped out of the shoe, clutching it in a fist. "I don't have friends." Her face burned. "I mean, don't call me Kirstie." Egads, if those women only knew what a mistake they'd made.

"I like Peppy better anyway." He reached over the railing with a hand out. "You're on time."

"I meant that my name is Kirsten. Not Kirstie or Peppy. I'm not Peppy." She bit her lip.

"Maybe you should stop hugging that shoe so hard. I might think you're nervous."

Heat prickled her chin. "I was supposed to meet a Captain Ricardo. A man with an accent."

His broad smile showed a row of pearly teeth. "He works for me." He tightened his bowtie, then leaned further over the railing, an arm outstretched again. "I can lower the ladder, but you're a spit of a thing. Come over here. I'll bring you aboard."

"You'll do no such thing." Shivering and sweating, Kirsten looked about the inky night, hoping she wasn't alone with this man.

"We're alone," he said.

Not wanting to take time to put on her shoe, she started a hop-along, half-barefoot retreat back up the pier toward her car.

"I'm Jonathon VanBrocklin. I own the topless fishing tour business. And you own a failing restaurant that you blame on me. Want to talk? The champagne is chilled."

The memory of the women clapping for her--of all things, clapping--got to her. She had to at least try negotiating with this man. Also, a part of her feared Tootsie Winters' retaliation. It wasn't Kirsten's embarrassment that mattered if others found out the Peplinski women's history. It was her mother's health at stake. The doctors had been adamant: no stress.

"Okay, Mr. VanBrocklin, I'll come aboard. But no champagne. This is a business meeting." She looked at her watch, noticing her hand quaking. "I'll give you forty-five minutes."

"The stroke of midnight, agreed, we stop talking business."

The way he said that--and with the moon smiling over his shoulder--gave her pause. But she couldn't bear letting the owner of a nudie boat get the best of her.

He hauled her off the pier and into his arms so fast she gasped. She landed snug against his chest, her navy shoe clutched in her hands separating them. Her gaze met with a smooth, square chin and firm lips twitching enticingly not an inch from her own. Her heart sputtered worse than a robin in a birdbath. She breathed in a heady brew of aftershave and garlic. Garlic?

"Are you cooking something?" She sniffed the air, craning her neck toward the open cabin door.

"I thought you might enjoy my catch of the day. But then, I already have that in my arms."

She swallowed hard, pushing free to shake the shoe at him. "Mr. VanBrocklin, I'm here for discussion only."

"Perfect. I'm eager to get your opinion on my new recipe for apricot-stuffed trout with fresh green beans."

Her curiosity betrayed her. "I've never tried apricot. It's not too sweet with the fish?"

His broadening smile lured her. "The only thing sweet with my fish will be you."

"Mr. VanBrocklin, I'm not on anybody's menu--"

"Call me Jonathon." His sweeping arm signaled the awaiting cabin. "At least take a peek before you get upset. Tell me if my tastes are off."

A war gurgled inside her. Go in? Leave? The nervous gurgle came again, loud enough for him to hear.

He canted his head. "The trout is seared to a crisp brown at the edge. With butter."

The man was smooth, but she'd had plenty of practice over the years with cons herself. The thought brightened her. She could handle a tuxedo and trout. She'd show him who could con whom.

Clutching her shoe, Kirsten strolled unevenly into the cabin.

Chapter 3

Kirsten blinked at the unexpected accoutrements for a tart ship.

The predominantly white cabin, quiet and swaying on the water, could hold fifty guests easily. Only a few feet away from where she stood in the doorway, a glass-topped table reflected the chandelier above it. Chairs covered in white velveteen with satin trim glowed. A large painting at the far end of the room beyond a pool table and bar depicted the Wisconsin wilderness meeting the Lake Superior shoreline. Sconces along the walls dripped with crystals in the shape of--

"Those are fish?"

"Specially made in Corning, New York, in the artisan glass shops. Six types of fish commonly found in this area, including trout, perch, bluegill. Our dinner's getting cold."

The table settings looked fit for a White House dinner. When the boat rocked, the chandelier showered everything with sparkling confetti.

Jonathon pulled out a chair for her, his pearly smile beseeching. Her spine twitched at the uneasy notion of being on his menu. After slipping off her other shoe and setting the shoes aside, she padded across soft, white carpeting, then allowed him to seat her. He shook out the napkin to settle it in her lap, smoothing it with long fingers. The temperature in the room went up.

While serving from the chafing dishes nearby, he chatted about the weather, how he thought they'd get rain tonight and how he loved rain. The trout had a heady, buttery, apricot essence rising from the caramelized skin. Her mouth watered, darn him. The whiff of garlic she'd smelled earlier came on stronger with cloves of it tossed among bright green string beans.

He poured water from a silver pitcher. "I'll keep the champagne on ice, in case you change your mind." After settling in, he toasted with a water goblet. "Thank you for coming aboard."

She wanted to remind him that she asked to meet with him, not the other way around, but his blue eyes rocked her. Or was that the boat? Raising her glass revealed how much she was shaking, but she muscled it out. "So far, your recipe looks like a winner."

After her first bite into the apricot glazed trout with wild rice and apricot stuffing, she was lost again in those deep, blue eyes staring at her with an anxious hunger.

He winked. "What do you think?"

The hell with her pride. "I'd like to ask your permission to serve this at my restaurant."

"What's mine is yours."

Again an odd feeling crept over her. She had to remember this was all a con, and she had to con him right back. "Moonstone has a deal that I believe you can't refuse."

"Do you think the combination of the garlic in the beans with the sweetness of the trout's apricot glaze is too much?"

There he was again, rocking the atmosphere. "No, the garlic is sweet in its own way. It marries well with the tart apricot."

"Marries?" The way his face came alive--eyebrows rising, one corner of his mouth twitching, eyes twinkling--gave her pause again.

She reached for her water glass. "'Marrying' is a cooking term. You didn't crush the cloves, so it's not overpowering."

He sat back in triumph. "Oh hallelujah. Breaking in new chefs always takes a while. Tony will be happy to hear you said that."

She put down her fork, feeling like a fool. "This is what your babes will be serving the men of Moonstone tomorrow, won't they? You're having me help you test your recipes?"

"But I just agreed to share it. The recipe is yours now."

"So we'd both be using it. That would mean I'd be condoning you while competing with you." Slapping the napkin on the table, she shot up.

"Please, you're right," he said. "Competition in marriages is bad."

"What're you talking about?"

"You know more about cooking than I do. It's all yours. I won't use the recipe. I quit." The man looked panicked, his face pinker.

Kirsten's surprising victory was short-lived. As she eased into her chair, a grin crept onto his face as he dove into another bite of stuffed trout.

She tested him. "So you'll quit this nude fishing business? You'll move away from Moonstone?"

"What do you have against bare breasts?"

She got up, then marched out the cabin door--

--And discovered they were well out in Lake Superior.

The damn man had kidnapped her! He'd distracted her with his fancy food, fancy words and fancy, dreamy eyes! She fumbled in her pockets. No phone. She'd forgotten it in her other clothes.

She thought about stripping off the formal suit and trying to swim for the diminishing lights of the casino. But she suspected that was exactly what Jonathon VanBrocklin wanted--her in panties and bra.

She whipped around, her heart pounding. "Take me back."

"We haven't even broken up."

"Stop that. You're not funny."

After a shrug, he looked at his watch. "It's not midnight yet. You said we had until midnight."

She made fists. "Now! Take me back now!"

"See the clouds to the west covering the stars? There's a mist in the air. Where I'm from, we never have this kind of air. It's like cotton candy, so soft and thick you can almost eat it."

"Stop it. Stop trying to be romantic. I'm onto your charade. Mister, I can tell you I don't have a romantic bone in my body."

"Hmm. No friends and no romance. Quite the catch. Maybe I should toss you back in the water."

He wandered back inside, leaving her fizzing on deck. Toss her back? She'd been "tossed back" all her life. After sizing up the dangerous, brackish lake with its whitecaps, she headed inside on shaky knees for Round Two.

He lounged on a white leather sofa in a sitting area. Several robin's egg blue gift boxes with white bows nestled on the glass coffee table in front of him. He'd poured champagne in flutes. To her disgust, he grinned as if nothing had transpired between them. The eyes twinkled, luring her again-- as if she were a fish, which made her all the madder.

Trying to stomp, she failed with bare feet on the thick, white carpet. Affecting a pose, she peered down her nose. "I came to propose something."

"You're proposing to me?"

"Yes. No." Damn those eyes. "Okay, here's what we women want." *Those long arms around me, the lips on my...* Her grandmother had given her a speech to say. What was it? "Take this tub down to Lake Michigan, where you can park it near the beaches in Door County for rich Chicago people to use and lap up your trout. You're ruining our economy with your breasts."

Her face went scalding hot.

Over a sip of champagne, he mused, "Do you have anything else to threaten me with? Because that was quite confusing."

"I don't want you anywhere near my restaurant."

"With my breasts?"

She gave into a begrudging shrug. "I'm not good at giving speeches."

Leaning back, he stretched both arms across the back of the white sofa, then patted a cushion next to him. "Please sit. You're making me dizzy watching you sway with the boat, though there's an upside to such visions."

She wasn't about to sit anywhere near his "upside". She plunked into the white chair across the coffee table from him. "The men who get off your boat are acting like idiots. They party at all hours. Nobody's getting any business or sleep. I was sent here to save Moonstone."

"Sent by the women? Why?"

"They thought I would be the most reasonable. At least I wouldn't tie you up and pour honey on you and let the bears have their way with you."

"You have been polite. I like that about you."

She brightened.

Then his demeanor stiffened. "But I won't stop the fishing tours just because you're being ladylike." He glanced at his watch. "It's after midnight. No more business talk." He picked up one of the blue gift boxes, handing it across the coffee table. "For you."

"I don't want your bribes. I'm trying to threaten you."

"And I feel your fury. That's what I like about you, your courage."

"What courage?" She winced.

To her shock, he rounded the table, sunk to one knee in front of her to present the robin's egg blue gift box. "For you."

He had her trapped in the chair. Intent on ruining his game, she snatched the box, ripping off the wrapping and bow. "What is this, the key to your boat, I hope?"

She lifted off the box cover, then saw the word "Tiffany" on a ring box also in blue. Jonathon grinned up at her. "Will you--?"

She tossed the box at his head and scrambled over the back of the chair, dumping it. She fell with an oomph on the carpet, then crawled fast under the pool table. She stood up on the other side. "Where's the phone?" Frantic, she searched the bar, even looking in the refrigerator. "Where's your friggin' phone?"

Rubbing his head, Jonathon plucked the ring box from the floor. In swift steps he'd set it on the bar in front of her. She backed against a row of glasses that clinked behind her. Opening the box, he blinded her with a diamond that sparkled big as the chandelier. "Kirsten Peplinski, would you marry me?"

She dove from the bar to the sofa, grabbing a cushion to act as a shield. "Stay away from me with that ring."

He sauntered over, standing across the coffee table from her with the ring box open. The diamond--big as his pinkie--captured the chandelier's light and lured her attention again.

"You're proposing to me as a way to shut me up? To let you keep your boat?"

"I'm serious. I want you. We're perfect."

"You're perfectly insane." She edged her way down the sofa. "Where's Tony?"

"I gave him the night off."

There was still hope with Captain Ricardo. "I'll scream if you don't stop this."

"Captain Ricardo's discreet. He won't be interrupting us."

"Interrupting what?" The hairs on the nape of her neck lifted.

"I thought we'd talk about our wedding."

Maybe if she played along she could find a way to escape. "When are we, uh, getting, well you know, hitched?"

"I thought I'd let you pick the date since I've done a good portion of the other work already. I want you to feel comfortable about all this."

"Oh yeah, I'm comfortable," she said, trying to keep her balance as the boat rocked. Rain now beat against the windows.

"What's your favorite color?" he asked, righting the chair and sitting down. The ring sat sparkling on the coffee table.

"Why?"

"And favorite flower. Sunny yellow roses? We'll want to find a floral arranger who can ship them in fresh from the coast."

"Brown. I like brown and green," she said, "the color of land. Where I'd like to be."

Before she could blink he'd grabbed her cushion, tossed it aside and had her sitting next to him on the sofa. He took her hand in his strong, warm palm, sending bolts of hot panic through her. When he brought out the ring box, she whimpered.

The ring's marquis cut was lovely. It would accentuate her slim fingers.

She wanted to slap herself. She looked away. Her mistake. He slipped the ring on her finger.

"What--?"

His face leaned near hers, making her whimper again. "It matches the fire in your eyes, the intelligence waiting there that I wonder if people even bother to look for. I've been looking for that for a long time."

"I'm not marrying you." She slapped the ring back in his palm. "Have you been stalking me? How long is a long time?"

"Marry me and the boat goes. That's the deal. I don't stalk. I do research."

She blinked at him. He was serious! "I'm not in the marrying mood."

"The wedding will be a fairytale. I thought we'd have twelve bridesmaids and groomsmen."

"Twelve? I don't even know twelve women."

He began handing her the other gift boxes. "Oh, that's right. You said something earlier about not having friends. You'll have to start making some."

She pushed the boxes off her lap. "Get away from me with this crap."

He re-stacked boxes into her lap. "Those are the bridesmaid's gifts."

"You bought gifts for women I don't even know?"

"That will change. You're the mayor of Moonstone. You'll do a lot of glad-handing."

"Interim mayor. *Interim.* I don't need to get to know anybody. I'm temporary."

"Seems bad for business. Shouldn't a restaurant owner get to know her customers, make them feel at home, encourage them to come back again? Permanently?"

"If you're staying, I'm closing."

"You may want to stay close to home with our children, but we can hold off on having kids until we get to know each other better."

"How completely generous of you."

"You should really open those. I found the perfect gift for your bridesmaids. I think you'll be impressed."

He got up to pour champagne for her. She downed it in one gulp. This had to be a nightmare. She'd wake up soon.

Settling next to her again, he grinned with that unbearable twinkle in the blue eyes. He seemed completely, utterly sincere and happy--certifiable. Maybe it would be wise to humor him until they returned to shore.

Kirsten opened the boxes. Each held a different oval, white gem pendant. The smooth stones featured different patterns of delicate gray-blue veins that made them look like the face of the man in the moon. A silver design around each gem made it look as if hands held the moon.

"What are they?" she asked, a rush of heat at their beauty overwhelming her.

"Moonstones. I got them in India."

The intimate way his smile slid her way, creating a dimple, made her insides turn feathery. "You went to India to buy twelve necklaces. For me."

"You're worth it. And I took a Harry Potter book along. Read the whole thing on the flight."

Again, his casual sincerity rattled her. "Am I supposed to know you? Did you sit beside me in botany class? Oh crap, you weren't that pervert with the knee he always jiggled against mine?"

Jonathon got up to refill her champagne glass. "No. I'm a stock broker. I like fishing, hunting, and sailing. I grew up in Arizona. I've been thinking about retiring and switching careers."

"Retiring?" He couldn't be more than thirty-five.

"Thirty-six," he said, reading her look. "You're twenty-five. An eleven-year difference. But I'm in good shape. I'll keep up with you...in every way."

Heat dilly-dallied with her womanly parts.

He went on. "We have a lot in common. You were on the dean's list. So was I. We're both left-handed." He used his left hand to hand her the champagne flute.

"How do you know so much about me?"

"The Internet."

That gave her a chill. She knew about web pages that posted tax dodgers, pedophiles, and repeat drunk drivers. Were other types of pages posted now? Did he know everything?

She eased into her verbal stalking. "So what are your plans for Moonstone?"

"I was thinking of putting a dome over it."

She choked. "A bubble over the village?"

"The downtown square." He sat in the white chair. "We could add a pool to the park. The dome would draw tourists year round, even winter, when

I've heard it can get pretty dead up here. We'd want to fix up the historical buildings. We'd expand your restaurant."

"I don't own it. I manage it."

"What would you do with it if you did own it?"

Maybe it was the fuzz in her head from the champagne, but his idea intrigued her. "I was hoping to someday put a deck in the back facing the lake."

"Just a deck? Come on, think bigger." He came over to sit beside her, energy humming off him. Every hair follicle on her body bent his way, betraying her. "What about a conservatory? Where flowers bloom year-around and birds fly among the trees? A magic garden."

"I don't need magic."

He leaned closer, making her want to dive into his eyes. "Magic. That's what I'm feeling between us."

The humming grew louder. "You can stop now."

His lips brushed her ear. "I love your hair."

She was broiling, no freezing, no, gone hot all over. "It's a crappy cut on me."

"I like short hair on a woman. You look sassy." Firm, commanding lips slipped to her cheek, nuzzling a path toward her mouth.

The feathers inside her were now having a full-blown pillow fight of fun, inviting him to play.

His lips found her lips. He tasted of champagne and temptation.

Jonathon held her firm against him, one hand slipping into her hair, mussing it while he kissed her in a way that made her go liquid down to her bare toes. She should be pushing away, but what had she told him? She was interim. Temporary. This would all go away in a flash and she'd be safe again, alone and safe.

When he pushed her jacket down off her shoulders, she welcomed the cool effect, then did the unthinkable. She undid his bowtie.

It unleashed something in him. The next kiss brought them floundering about the sofa, a hunger grabbing them. She grabbed hold of his thick hair to bring him even closer.

He kissed her harder, whispering, "Sassy."

He managed to unbutton the top button of her crisp white blouse.

She tore at his shirt placket, exposing a tanned chest, revealing the broad shoulders that had held the moon. Her world rocked--

Then dumped them on the floor.

"Oh!" she yelped, rolling on top of him, her body recognizing his pressing need.

She shot off him, buttoning her blouse with shaky fingers. "You're trying to get me in a compromising position."

"Of course. We're a perfect match." He struggled up, hair mussed in a roguish way that sent her heart into first gear again.

She raced for the cabin door.

"Wait, Peppy, where're you going?"

"For a swim."

Outside, rain lashed her, but oddly enough she could see the bright lights of the casino. Jonathon had turned around long ago! He'd only made her think he'd kidnapped her.

"Come inside," he said, "and we'll get the wet clothes off you."

"I don't think so." The pier ebbed closer.

"When should we meet again? To talk over our wedding details?"

She trotted across the deck, grabbed the rail, and jumped.

Chapter 4

Kirsten sank against the kitchen door, dripping, a hand over her pounding heart. Her grandmother stood in the archway to the living room looking dumbfounded. Kirsten puffed out, "Thank goodness it's you and not Mom. She'd have another heart attack over this lunatic I just escaped from."

"She's sound asleep. New meds. He's loony how?"

Grandma Tracy clicked into the kitchen on red mule slippers, wearing baby doll pajamas spattered with red hearts and red ostrich feathers floating about the hem. Kirsten liked her grandmother's youthfulness, but sometimes reminders of the old days worried her.

Water droplets slid down Kirsten's face and off her nose. "He wants to marry me."

With a sly grin, Grandma Tracy handed over a dish towel from the stove rung. "Is he handsome?" She swished to the table to sit down, almost disappearing behind Kirsten's mother's birdhouses.

Ellen Peplinski had discovered the high art of birdhouse making, painting them in patchwork colors. She also applied doo-dads of all kinds with a glue gun. Kirsten didn't dare drop a barrette for fear it'd end up glued to a birdhouse roof. But birdhouse making had reduced Ellen's blood pressure and that was all that mattered to Kirsten.

"This was business, remember? I've forgotten his looks already."

When Kirsten padded over to the stove to hang the wet towel, her grandmother asked, "What happened to your shoes?" Then-- "Ohhhhh."

"We discussed money, not sex," Kirsten said, wriggling out of the wet suit jacket.

"Sure, dear. Now tell me the real story of what happened to your shoes."

Kirsten hung her jacket over the back of a chair. "I sacrificed them for the cause."

"Go back and get them, Cinderella."

"They're only shoes." She stripped out of the wet slacks, sitting down in her soggy blouse and underwear across from her grandmother.

Grandma Tracy shoved birdhouses aside. "Those are the last shoes I got for you before all the business."

Kirsten froze. "I've been wearing stolen shoes? When did you do that?"

"Day before I went to prison. Italian leather worth five hundred dollars. They were on sale for three-fifty. The store was crowded. The clerk left that box on the floor amid all the other boxes and I couldn't help myself. It was like a last cigarette before finally breaking the habit."

Kirsten's insides--her hope for them going straight--shattered like glass. "You haven't stolen anything else, have you?"

"Of course not, honey." But Kirsten didn't like the way her grandmother averted her gaze while fingering buttons glued on a birdhouse roof. "I'm surprised you're back so early."

"You expected me to stay the night?"

Her grandmother shrugged. "Those women in Moonstone expect results. Why else would they have chosen you?"

Shrinking into self-doubt, Kirsten said, "You think they picked me because they think I'm easy? Do they know about us? That darn Tootsie Winters--"

"Forget Tootsie. I'm sure she kept her promise to the grant committee not to say anything. Honey, they chose you because there's a light in your eyes, a spark that says you can figure your way out of any kind of trouble."

Kirsten wanted to believe that.

Her grandmother reached between the birdhouses to pat her hands. "Now get to the good stuff."

But Kirsten kept the good stuff to herself, putting the memory of Jonathon's kiss into an imaginary robin's egg blue box to hoard deep within her heart. She told Grandma Tracy about the moonstones.

"Twelve? With man in the moon faces? Do you know how much we could get for those? Go back and say 'yes'."

Terror struck Kirsten. "Stay away from that boat, you hear me, Grandma?"

"I'm just funnin' ya." Leaning forward, she whispered, "Do you think he might be serious?"

"Oh he's serious. He said the boat is staying put."

"No, about wanting to marry you."

"I don't know anything about him!"

"Right there, that's your problem. You went into that lion's den without a scrap of research, no weapons on you. I bet he knew a lot about you."

Self-doubt turned into nausea. Grandmother was right. Kirsten had always been this way. She could be bossed around, always the follower and never the leader or "thinker". What did she know about Jonathon? With a dimply smile he talked about putting magic in her life. Tootsie was right, too. She was a ninny in a funny hat. A dunce.

With awakening dread over meeting with the women, she pushed up from the table. "I'm going to bed. Tomorrow's my public flogging."

"Now none of that, Missy Mayor. You'll think of something to tell the gals. You've got that spark. Just look in the mirror if ever you feel down."

But her failed life bubbled up, drowning her. She couldn't recall a single success in her life. Even graduating from college had been at a judge's behest. She dragged herself to the hallway staircase.

Grandma Tracy toddled after her. "Isn't it ironic that he'd buy all those moonstones? Moonstones are known for healing emotional wounds, for creating love. I wonder what about his past he's trying to heal?"

"But the moonstones were for me and my wedding."

Her grandmother's hand was a tender vise on Kirsten's wrist. "It's rare to find a true romantic these days in such a rude world. Was it love at first sight, dear?"

"I'm not in love with him." *A secret kiss held within my heart is not love! Who would want to love a ninny?*

"Did his moonstones give you a flutter? You forgot your shoes. Did you forget your head?"

"Don't be silly." But everything about Jonathon had made her pause, giving her tiny vacations from real life. The taste of his firm lips lingered with her, making her heart...

She wagged a finger at her grandmother. "Nice try. You just want those expensive shoes back, don't you?"

"Whatever." Grandma Tracy winked. "What is it that you want?"

On Saturday morning, Kirsten struggled into baggy, khaki shorts and a sleeveless, pink cotton blouse she tied at the waist. She hoped sweet pink would win her some pity. The pink reminded her of Margie. A wistful tug hit

Kirsten. What if her grandmother's assessment was correct about her and the spark in her eyes? What if she could somehow wave a magic moonstone around and fix things so that Margie could finally go on a blind date and find true love?

Now who was the romantic!

At The Jingle Bell Inn she softened up the women by preparing a special luncheon of cold raspberry soup, chicken breasts rolled around cream cheese and dandelion leaves, with a raspberry sauce drizzled on top. Dessert was homemade chocolate chip cookie ice cream. She served iced tea with mint leaves from the mansion's refurbished garden patches.

Tootsie Winters called the meeting to order, then returned to her chair, picking at a piece of dandelion leaf that had dropped on her bosom. "He came to his senses, right?"

Leaning for support on the hostess station, all that Kirsten could think about in looking across the small crowd of women was a stupid question: Which twelve would she choose for the moonstone necklaces?

Wringing her apron, she began babbling about what the boat looked like, hoping they'd be distracted from her failure to get rid of the thing.

Jeri said, "The chairs were white velveteen? He's never had to deal with children during flu season."

Giggles rippled through the room.

"He has his own chef out there?" Margie asked in disbelief. "The least he could do is buy supplies from my IGA."

"He has a chandelier?" asked Lily, fingering her pearls. "The only other one we have in Moonstone is here at the North Pole."

So far, so good. But Kirsten's brain insisted on counting. She knew Jeri, Marge, and Lily. Only nine more to go. Why didn't she have friends? She grabbed for a glass of ice water.

Crystal raised her hand from the back of the room. "What did you talk about?"

Four. Only eight more women to go. "We...talked about food."

Rita hooted, "Good idea. Food is the way to a man's stomach."

Five. *Take that Jonathon VanBrocklin! I have friends aplenty!*

But Rita persisted. "Did you cook for him? Bribe him with your recipes?"

Heat scored Kirsten's face. "He had his own recipe, and an invitation of sorts."

Lily, dressed in a maroon suit with lipstick to match popped up from her chair. "He's not inviting us to his boat, is he? I won't be seen on that thing unless it starts raining for forty days and nights and he's got two of every animal."

Margie tossed out, "He probably does, but don't ask what he does with them."

The women giggled again. Kirsten bit her lip against heat rising as she recalled tumbling on the carpet with Jonathon like two animals in heat.

Jeri said, "I don't care if this man is Noah, Moses, or George Clooney. My husband's gone fishing again today and I want Mr. VanBrocklin to part the waters and leave. You gave him a deadline, right?"

Kirsten burned hotter. She hadn't thought of that.

Comely Lily said, "You were supposed to strike a deal. The issue was money, remember? The bank has no money because all the businesses have no money. The men aren't working and the customers aren't coming...well, sort of they are."

Kirsten's stomach gurgled. "He wants to put a dome over Moonstone."

The collective "What?!" made her squeak fast, "He said it would bring more tourists and money."

Tootsie waddled to the front of the room. "You didn't offer him Moonstone in exchange for that nudie boat?"

"No," Kirsten peeped, her brain counting again. Tootsie would make six. No way. She subtracted Tootsie. "He said he'd enclose the square, make the park useable year round. He mentioned a swimming pool. None of us can afford a swimming pool." *Oh my gosh, I'm turning into his ambassador.*

Amid the grumbling, Rita raised her hand again. "I've delivered mail when it's forty-below here. Maybe that's not such a bad idea."

Kirsten drank more ice water. Had she counted Rita? Yes, she had. She was still at six women that she barely knew--if she had to stoop to inviting Tootsie to her wedding. Pitiful. *Why don't I have any friends?*

A woman from the back piped up, "It'd get the kids out of the house in winter. They drive me nuts with their fighting."

Possible "friend" material? The other woman at the same table nodded. "Our kids would be gone all weekend and we'd finally have free time. I say if he's willing to shut down his tours and run the water park instead for the kids that we go for it."

Kirsten died inside. Jonathon hadn't been willing to stop his tours at all. "Ladies, remember why we love Moonstone. It's small and quiet, lovely in its own way, and--" What? *Think!* "It smells good."

They stared at her, stunned, but she kept on. "Yes, it smells pretty darn good around here. You don't need those little pine tree air fresheners for your cars because of all the pines we have. You just roll down the windows to blow any stink off your kids or husbands."

Nobody laughed.

Swallowing, she explained, "If you turned this into a water park year-round, you'd have even more traffic than we have now--stinky exhaust fumes--and trash to pick up."

"Trash?" scoffed Tootsie. "We'd have jobs for our teenagers finally."

Lily fingered her pearls. "I'm impressed, Kirsten. The dome will boost our economy, and we'll be rid of the tart boat at the same time. When do you meet with this guy next?"

The women looked up at her from their seats. *Think! Be a leader!*

"I'm...meeting with him again tonight." *He just doesn't know it.*

This time she vowed there'd be no kisses mussing up the discussion. She was stronger now; she could feel her leadership skills soaring.

At eleven o'clock, Kirsten showed up on the pier in Port Cliff. Despite the balmy seventy-five-degree summer night, and the hot zones alive within her body, she shivered in her khaki shorts and pink blouse.

Jonathon leaned a bare chest over the railing. "Hey, gorgeous."

Moonlight glistened off his pecs and shoulders. Kirsten itched in places she couldn't scratch.

He waved a notepad. "I've made a list of my favorite songs for the processional of your bridesmaids. Come aboard, Peppy."

The breeze tossed his hair about in an erratic way that matched her heartbeat. "I came to... I need my shoes back."

Jonathon's laughter rumpled the stars overhead. "I suspect you asked for this meeting for something far more serious than shoes."

Drying her perspiring hands against her shorts, she said, "I'm here for the women."

"So you found twelve bridesmaids?"

"I found a town full of women ready to sue you because their marriages are falling apart."

"Because their men *choose* to go fishing."

"That's a choice? Dangling...stuff?"

"Dangling beauty in front of them makes them choose my fishing boat over your restaurant. That's what bothers you. Maybe you need a nudie show if the food isn't luring them in."

She shook a fist at him. "You're vile."

"Ah, so you've finally looked me up online." His smile matched the moon's.

Why didn't I take the time to look at the moon before? How could you not smile back at the moon? Why did it feel so good to do so?

He said, "I absolutely believe in destiny, hunches, instinct and love at first sight."

She'd only found articles online about his financial deals. To her consternation, the man appeared more virile than vile. But love at first sight? Her body itched again, warning her that he liked playing games. "You're a broker, not a matchmaker. Hunches and instinct work for buying stock, but not for love."

"So you believe that love has to be planned out? Like arranged marriages?"

"Yes. No." Egads, he had her spinning again. "If I can't make you leave, I'm going to have to close my restaurant. You've ruined me with your 'choices'."

The dimple in his cheek disappeared. "Sometimes things in the stock market take a temporary dip, a correction, and then they come back even stronger. I sense that's you."

"No, Jonathon. Thanks for ruining me, my family, and Moonstone." She did an about-face.

"Wait. I asked Tony to hang around tonight. I wanted to show you the latest recipe he got from the Wynn Hotel in Las Vegas where he trained. Recipes he made for top entertainers."

Blast. Visions of customers--movie stars--flying in from the coasts to try her recipes learned from the Wynn Hotel's kitchen assailed her. She let Jonathon hoist her onto the yacht. Landing with her hands planted on his firm, warm plains of flesh, she felt like a helpless fish sizzling in his frying pan already. Jonathon smelled of soap--clean and delectable. Now even her tongue itched. "I suppose you know Steve Wynn."

"He's invited to our wedding."

"Of course," she said, battling a smile that would only encourage him.

To her surprise, none of it was a lie. He introduced Tony Farina, a short, dark, rail-thin, fiftyish man wearing the requisite white uniform and toque.

Tony tied long aprons on them, plunging them elbow deep in the making of a puff pastry stuffed with native wild mushrooms. The heady perfumes of cloves, basil, and butter created a red aura around them.

To roll out dough, Jonathon playfully wrapped his bare arms around her, his hands clasping over the top of hers. His cheek--the one with the dimple--settled on hers as he jiggled her in a dance while crooning like Wayne Newton. Her hands slipped off the rolling pin, up-ending a cup of flour nearby. It exploded into their faces, even Tony's. All three stared at each other, looking like ghosts.

Kirsten flushed with embarrassment. "I'm sorry. I, uh--" Oh crap, what to say? "I'm used to working alone. And not dancing with rolling pins."

When Tony broke into laughter along with Jonathon, she burst into giggles, too. They swabbed at their faces with their apron skirts. "I'll pay for the flour," she offered.

Tony shook his head, pouring them all a glass of Italian red wine. "There's a little store in the village I've yet to explore. I'll go in search of flour tomorrow."

Jonathon toasted. "It was my fault. I shouldn't be caught in a kitchen with these clumsy things." He showed off a large hand. "I'll watch from now on and leave cooking to you experts."

Kirsten basked in the compliment. They dove into making a coconut encrusted shrimp favored by a famous actor. Next, Tony showed her how to make salmon with a crushed pepper crust over steamed cabbage leaves, which a certain rap star craved obsessively.

"You know both of them, too, don't you?" she asked of Jonathon, who now worked as her own personal clean-up staff, washing pans and utensils.

"Only the rap star. Our firm handles his investments. I could invite him to perform at your restaurant."

"No, thank you." She couldn't imagine the conservative, Lutheran farmers around Moonstone eating their Friday fish fry to pulsating rap music.

Tony left around one in the morning after writing down the recipes for her. She waved goodbye from the deck, then turned to find herself in Jonathon's arms. He still wore the white apron over his bare chest. "I want to show you the stars."

She giggled, reaching out to rub his earlobe. "Flour."

When Jonathon took her hand in his and kissed her knuckles, the moon--peeking over his shoulder again--seemed to wink at her. The man in the moon knew she was falling for the comfort of the strong arms around her, the scent of soap and skin, and the promise of playfulness and pleasure that defined Jonathon in whatever he did.

She stepped back, breathing in the night air off the lake to clear her head.

"What's wrong?" he asked.

"Just a shooting star surprising me." *Just a yearning turning me to mush.*

"I can't believe the stars here. There're so many of them."

"We make them in a factory here in Moonstone."

He chuckled. She liked the sound. She liked having an influence over him.

Leaning in, giving her a close-up of the soft hue of his eyes, he said, "I had fun tonight. Best date I've ever had."

"I thought this was a meeting," she said, scrounging for the strength to escape.

"You have flour on your face, too. Right here."

His breath tickled her cheek, then his tongue flicked out, tasting her. "We seem to have a lot of flour to clean up yet. This could take all night."

He claimed her lips with a hunger, pulling her hard against him. The stars spun in the sky. The moon politely turned his head. Kirsten melted into Jonathon's heat, feeling a release rush through her, a letting go of all her worries, flaws, and anxiety over not ever saying the right thing. Now, her body was speaking in perfect sentences and Jonathon was completing them with sizzling punctuation.

The boat rocked. No, it was Jonathon lifting her in his arms.

Taking her inside.

Taking her.

On his big, fluffy bed. They chased across a cloud, tasting and tickling, hanging onto stars, skipping to their heartbeats, drifting into pleasure. And danger.

Chapter 5

Kirsten woke startled at the first seepage of sunlight. A heat wave broke over her at the memory of last night. Jonathon VanBrocklin had proven to have Viking ways, capturing and plundering.

Her stomach gurgled. She held her breath. Jonathon didn't awaken. She had the urge to smooth the hair off his forehead, to let a thumb linger on the relaxed crease where the dimple always formed.

After pulling on her clothes, she hurried to her car. In fumbling in her shorts' pockets for the car keys, she discovered his note.

"Tell the ladies of Moonstone I plan to court you properly, and on the day of our wedding, the topless touring boat gets dry-docked. P.S. Tiffany's is re-sizing the ring. It slipped off your finger too easily. It will be here in three days."

Kirsten wanted to stamp her feet and scream, but that would wake him. Instead, she drove fast down the highway with the windows open to the crisp, pine-scented air. A glance in the rearview mirror showed lips lush from lovemaking. She had a goofy grin on her face like Crystal's. A vision of plump

Tootsie in a Tiffany blue, poufy-sleeved bridesmaid dress thrust her into panic mode.

Yet again she'd failed in her mission. Some mayor she made. Her wayward reactions to Jonathon had to stop. She couldn't be cozying up to his gems or his family jewels. Men were missing because of the boat she'd just had sex on.

Wait a minute, that's it. Sexy fun was something the Peplinski women were experts at, so why not use sex to solve her problems? Just like that, a plan to get rid of Jonathon popped into her head.

Then a big, fat dollop of doubt hit her like a bug splatting on the windshield. Her plan could lead to revelations about her nefarious past and run her family out of town once more. She couldn't do that to her mother and grandmother. But what if she took charge this time, instead of her grandmother and mother? After all, it was their little plans--not hers--that had led to them all wearing jailhouse jewelry.

When Kirsten looked into the mirror again she saw a new spark in her eyes. Somehow she had found courage. She shuddered to think it might have come about because she'd made love with Jonathon. With heat riddling her, she turned on the car's air conditioning.

She had to make this work. The ladies of Moonstone expected her to save them. Heck, she had to save herself, too. There was no way she wanted Jonathon inside her restaurant on bended knee in three days with that flashy diamond ring from Tiffany's. No way. What woman would want that?

Later that Sunday morning Kirsten gathered the women at her restaurant. Her courage almost slipped as she assessed the conservative bunch wearing dresses and pantyhose--even with sandals--in the hot weather. Did she dare propose her plan?

She took a deep breath. "He's tough. I failed to threaten him."

Grumbling erupted. Wrong start. Kristen swallowed. *Why didn't I take forensics? Who cared that the teacher didn't wear deodorant and also taught gym? Why did he also have to make us climb the rope to the gym ceiling? What was that all about?*

Rita spoke first. "There wasn't a man except the preacher in my church this morning. And I swear he was rushing through the sermon so he could go fishing. We have to do something."

Tootsie asked, "Did you negotiate anything at all?"

"I spent all night negotiating--"

"All night?" Tootsie's gaze pierced Kirsten.

Lily touched her pearls. "You spent the night with him?"

Margie's bosom warred against her blouse when she shot up. "She didn't just talk! She's glowing!"

"I am?" Kirsten felt like a boat anchor sinking fast.

"You are, oh my God, we're ruined," rippled through the room.

There was only one way out of this: the truth of his plan and her counter-plan. "He wants me to marry him."

"What?!" went the chorus.

"If I marry him, then he'll close down the boat." Her armpits were raining.

Tootsie clapped. "An easy solution. Congratulations."

"I'm not marrying Jonathon VanBrocklin."

"Maybe you could date him for a while, butter him up," dreamy-eyed Crystal offered.

Kirsten straightened her shoulders. "What if, ladies, all of you could have your men back, totally devoted to you, bringing you gifts, giving you foot rubs?"

"He gave you a foot rub?" Tootsie asked.

"No, but think about--"

"Did he give you gifts? Bribes?"

Kirsten sank further. "He wanted to give me moonstones."

"Good ones with man in the moon faces?" Lily asked. "Those should be in my vault for safekeeping."

Jeri puddled up, odd for the no-nonsense bus driver. "Moonstones for the mayor of Moonstone. That's poetic."

"I'm interim mayor! Temporary. Forget me. I'm just the worm you put on the hook to catch the man. Think about you, about your men giving you foot rubs while they're dressed only in an apron, and cooking for you..."

The women blinked in shock. A few blushed.

"Only an apron? Now that's one heck of a blind date," Margie said. "I'm in. What else ya got?"

They leaned forward in their chairs.

⚜

After a shopping trip to Superior and Duluth that afternoon, the women transformed the village. They kept shops open late. They put up flags and balloons on light poles. Kirsten cooked Tony's delectable Las Vegas recipes. She hammered in a sign in the mansion's front lawn: "Tonight's feature: Homemade Angelina Jolie saucy sauce."

The first run of men off the tart boat came in around six-thirty. The July humidity carried the scent of their boozy carousing. Instead of admonishing husbands and boyfriends, the women were instructed by Kirsten to coo and compliment. It'd taken some doing teaching Tootsie how to coo instead of bray, but Kirsten had reminded her of the possible foot rubs from her husband.

After staggering out of their trucks, the men stopped, eyeballs popping. Some had tongues lolling out.

Women of all shapes strutted about town wearing nothing but bustiers and short-shorts, or itsy bitsy bikinis, Kirsten among them. Her red, sequined bikini sparkled like a French spinner charming a hapless guppy. Brakes screeched. Word spread fast. Husbands raced to find their wives, then didn't know what to do with them.

Greg Johnson entered the hardware store to see his wife, Rita, in spike heels and scraps of lacey cloth filling a bag with fishing lures for a man forking over cash with a silly grin.

Men buying snacks at the IGA bought even more snacks so they could go through the line again to see Margie's 44-D's flopping about in a yellow bikini top in front of the checkout scanner. It was hard to tell if the hundred-dollar total ringing up was for food or her boobs. Margie winked. Men adjusted their stances and wallets.

In the park, men gawked at the trim and muscled Jeri in her leopard-print halter top and thong playing a charity volleyball game with other women bouncing in teeny-weeny outfits. Donation cups inside a bra on a table filled rapidly for the school's library.

A new side to the women--even Tootsie--flowered in their instant stardom. "I'm finally cool! The hell with menopause! No clothes, no hot flashes!"

Kirsten made an exception for her own attire in the restaurant, donning her full, white apron over the red bikini. But she, too, felt free to leave her shy demeanor behind. She decided to get to know her customers in a meaningful way. In the kitchen she wrote notes to help her remember them: *Jake had a mole removed. His wife, Ella Mae, used to teach science at the high school. Their twin daughters, Francie and Freddie, are my age and are itching to start an interior design company. (I think they're the ones in the matching purple bikinis.) Ben is a third-generation sheep farmer, had a hip replaced. His wife Betty asked me to come out to see the wool felt purses she makes.*

When Kirsten got home that night, Grandma Tracy tisked. "This is going to backfire. This is too close to the old days."

But success buoyed Kirsten. "It's harmless. No money's changing hands except for the men spending gobs of money now in Moonstone instead of on that boat."

On Monday, The Jingle Bell Inn's lunchtime crowd swelled. She could barely keep up, so she snagged a couple of gawking high school boys, pressing them into service as waiters.

Word had gotten out fast about the shapely, sexy women of Moonstone. That morning, a radio disc jockey mentioned the misbehavin' in Moonstone.

At the bank, men lined up to catch a peek at Lily. The conservative woman was short enough behind the teller counter that in her strapless tank top and no pearls, she looked naked. Deposits at the bank broke a record by noon. Even people driving through town stopped to open accounts.

When Jonathon appeared at the restaurant's hostess stand during the lunch rush, Kirsten was sure her skin matched the red bikini under her apron. The yacht owner looked dapper in a white polo shirt stretched across the broad shoulders. He wore black shorts, showing off tanned legs. Wind had whipped attitude into his hair.

"May I..." *May I comb your hair with my fingers and kiss you right here in front of everybody and--?* "May I seat you, sir?"

He took a gander about the room. That was when she noticed the dimple was gone. "The recipes appear to be popular."

"Thank you." Was he jealous of her sudden success? "I tweaked them, made them my own."

"There aren't any customers for the boat rides. Tony got to take the day off."

So he *was* upset at her success. Kirsten offered a smile. "I should hire Tony. My business has picked up."

His meandering gaze assessing her body caused a stir in her middle. "All of this is your idea?"

She liked the confusion galloping across his face. "You might as well motor that boat on down to Chicago or anywhere but here."

"That would mean reneging on my promise."

"What promise?"

"I said three days. I'm courting you for three days to prove we're perfect for each other. This is war."

A fissure cracked her confidence. "The women of Moonstone aren't quitting after three days. We mean to get our man, no matter how hard he is, it is, not his parts, that is, the war...that is hard, not the men...you." *Curses!*

Jonathon winked, his dimple smugly in place.

Sweating, she hurried to hide in the kitchen.

That Monday evening, Jonathon returned in his white tuxedo jacket and bowtie with a bouquet of red roses clutched in one fist and a little, dark-haired boy in the other. Kirsten saw danger blinking at her. After being introduced to Michael Lone Eagle, a very proud six going on seven, she pointed him toward the ice cream cone station at the end of the salad bar.

She seethed at Jonathon. "You borrowed a kid to make yourself look like husband material, like somebody everybody should like? You should be ashamed."

He waved the sweet-smelling bouquet under her nose. "His mother is the cook at the casino and she was called away on an emergency. Michael's father is a construction worker, been gone to New Orleans for a while. He fell through the roof of a house being repairing."

She wanted to crawl back to her kitchen. "I didn't know. Will his dad be okay?"

"Claire said he's got feeling in both legs, so that's a good sign."

Jonathon's gazed drifted to the tyke attempting to steady a third scoop of ice cream atop a waffle cone. Kirsten saw a softening on Jonathon's face, which made her feel all the worse for her accusation.

"You and Michael are staying for dinner. It's on me." She grabbed the roses. "These are lovely. Thank you."

His smile sent a betraying tickle to her middle. She led Jonathon and Michael to a table near the windows overlooking the flower beds and Lake Superior. After serving them her new Angelina Jolie saucy sauce on their burgers, she sneaked peeks from her kitchen door. Jonathon had the boy giggling, taking Michael's mind off his troubles.

Looking over at the roses on the counter, Kirsten sighed. Wasn't she supposed to be getting rid of Jonathon? Tootsie was right; she was too young to manage a business. She couldn't even manage her own heart.

By Tuesday afternoon, tourists crowded Moonstone. Booths had sprung up with locals selling everything from handmade Christmas ornaments to paintings of wolves and black bears. Kirsten was cutting across the park to pick up butter at the IGA when she spotted her mother at a table filled with birdhouses.

"Mom? This heat's not good for your heart. You should be home."

"Honey, I made three-hundred dollars already."

"Oh. Where's Grandma?" She was usually watching over Ellen.

"She said she had business. Perhaps grocery shopping."

"I'll ask her to bring you ice water. Please take it easy."

The IGA was so packed with men ogling women that Kirsten didn't see her grandmother. She grabbed the butter and squeezed between bodies to get to the checkout counter. Margie bounced up and down in excitement, her 44-D's threatening to trip the price scanner. "I met a man." Margie's eyes sparkled like crackle glass in sunlight. "Just like you. Love at first sight."

"I'm not in love." Kirsten rubbed perspiring palms on her bikini bottom.

"Jonathon says you are. He wanted to know who all your friends were. He was making a list."

Kirsten growled. "You told him you weren't my friend, didn't you?" She bit her lip at Margie's pained expression. "I'm sorry. Nothing I say comes out right. You know that, Margie. You're my friend. Really."

Margie leaned across the counter to smother her in a bosomy hug. "Friends." She was sniffling now. "Friends help each other be all they can be. Look at what you've done for me."

Kirsten hurried out, worried about the war. She couldn't let Jonathon show up with twelve women to ask for her hand in marriage in front of the entire town. But she was disappointed that he didn't show up at dinnertime. For Margie, she had to get rid of Jonathon. Margie deserved a man who didn't end up on the tart boat like all the other men of Moonstone.

At ten o'clock she closed up, changed into a fresh white blouse and denim skirt, then drove to the Port Cliff dock, intending on brokering a deal with Jonathon. If he didn't leave Moonstone, she would. She didn't see any alternative.

The sight of a squad car made her drive by. She pulled in after it left. "Jonathon?"

He popped his head over the railing, trouble wrinkling his face. "Bad news."

"Is Michael's dad all right?"

"As far as I know."

To her surprise Jonathon jumped over the railing, landing on the wood pier in front of her. "We have to delay the wedding." Distress had erased his dimple.

"Delay? What's wrong?" Her voice cracked with ridiculous concern.

"Your bridesmaids' gifts are gone."

"The moonstones were stolen?" Shivering, she knew where the moonstones were. "Maybe they slipped under a cushion of the couch. We were sort of active--"

She read the look on his face, then shriveled inside. "You told the cops I was one of the last people on the boat."

"I couldn't lie to a cop."

"Yes, you could!" Sweat prickled her face, even her nose, which was growing. "Why would I steal the moonstones when you gave them to me and I could just walk off with them with your blessing and sell them on the Internet or something?"

She fumbled harder. "If you loved me you would've lied about me. I mean, telling the truth isn't love. Love is all about lying to protect each other. I...lie to you all the time."

Stepping back from her, pain darkened Jonathon's face.

Feeling the sting of his disappointment, she got in her car and drove away fast.

Chapter 6

"Grandmother, how could you do this to me?" Kirsten leaned against the kitchen doorjamb to catch her breath. *What did I tell Jonathon?* She shivered under the fear that she'd somehow told him she loved him, which couldn't go anywhere for either of them, because she'd also hurt him.

The only light came from the open refrigerator. Grandma Tracy poured a glass of milk. She pointed at a new crop of birdhouses on the table. "Your mother said she made two hundred dollars selling her birdhouses today."

"Three hundred. She's holding out on you, but she learned it from you. Now cough up the moonstones."

"Of course you'd accuse me, but I forgive you." Grandma Tracy flounced in her babydolls to a chair at the table, fluttering her eyelashes. "So how do you know his moonstones are gone?"

"So how do you like his boat, which you sneaked on sometime when I wasn't watching you?"

"Not enough red for my taste. I was surprised there was no pole. I was kind of itching to try one again."

Kirsten slid into a chair. Moonlight cast the room in gray shadows, matching her mood. "Why did you do this?"

"Listen, honey, I didn't say I did anything but visit his boat. I was simply curious, for old time's sake."

"Somebody took the moonstones."

"And the mystery thief is doing you a favor. You don't want to marry him, right?"

"Of course not." The words tasted tainted, as if she'd bitten into a rotten apple. "He spent a lot of money on those jewels for me. I can't do this to him."

Grandma Tracy toasted with the milk glass. "Do I sense a softening toward him?"

"I'm soft in the head. The man makes me mad."

"Mad enough to wear a bikini in public. Mad enough to get your restaurant booming overnight. Mad enough to revitalize an entire dying town. That's an interesting madman."

"Grandma, he could have me put in jail."

"You don't have the moonstones, so the marriage is still on. He'll come around."

"Now you've changed your mind? You want me to marry him? I thought you were helping me get rid of him." Getting rid of Jonathon felt wrong--at least at this moment. She had to prove her innocence to him, had to give him back the moonstones. So he could give them to her again? She groaned, burying her head in her hands.

"Honey, love is like that," her grandmother said. "Flip-flops like a fish on a dock. You ask yourself constantly, shall I go in or stay out? I'd dive in. Fish get stinky when they stay out of the water too long."

"I can't love him. He's egotistical, doesn't listen, and he's...too smart and rich for me."

"Then why care about his damn moonstones?"

Because he's fun, kind, and takes a woman around the moon in bed?

Her grandmother tapped the table. "If I lifted the gems--if, that is--then I'm helping you. I bet he's so discombobulated he won't know what to do except leave. Voila! You're the town's heroine."

No, the pitiful virgin tossed into the lake. "He'll leave, but so will you, mom, and me. You're on parole, Grandma, and I signed a piece of paper promising not to be involved in anything like this again. You and I gave mom that heart attack. What do you think's going to happen if she gets wind of this? I'm hurting everybody."

Her grandmother flinched for the first time. "Who's everybody?"

"It's strange, but as much as Jonathon is different, he made me do things I like about myself. I have some dignity again."

"In that red bikini?"

"Yes. My plan was genius, Grandma. I did that for the other women. They're 'everybody'. I did it for them, with nothing in it for me. I risked everything for friendship for the first time in my life." Kirsten drew in a fortifying breath to ward off angry tears.

Grandma Tracy shrugged. "So marry him if he brings you dignity. There's nothing wrong with his money either. The man's filthy rich. I looked him up on his computer. Works for a big Arizona firm. Used to play on a college football team. A football team plus a coach makes twelve men, or groomsmen. He had them rounded up on an email list."

Kirsten rushed to the cupboard for aspirin. "There's no way he'd marry into this family. You're going to take those moonstones back."

"I don't have them, dear."

"You're taking them back and I'm helping you. I don't want you messing up again. Don't you dare go back there alone. We'll sneak on, put them under a cushion. We'll take cookies with us in case he catches us. He's babysitting a little boy. I'll say we brought cookies for Michael."

"That's another great plan, dear, right up there with the bikini show. Now if only I had the moonstones the plan would make sense. They say love blinds and you're proof of it."

The next morning, Kirsten and her grandmother did a "drive-by" of the yacht, despite her grandmother's protests about not having moonstones. Jonathon was polishing his deck, so they returned to town.

The place boomed. Another new business had started. Wearing a zebra-striped top and matching shorts, Tootsie led a bus load of elderly people on a tour. Jeri waved at Kirsten from the driver's seat of the bus, a wad of cash in hand.

Kirsten readied lunch while Grandma went home to bake oatmeal-butterscotch-raisin cookies. Ellen was safely away, having left for the park earlier with a wheelbarrow full of birdhouses. The restaurant featured a salad bar today. If Kirsten left for half an hour to sneak moonstones back in place, she could trust the two high school boys to shuffle people through the salad bar. While filling the lettuce bin, hair on the back of her neck tickled.

Jonathon was waving at her from outside the sliding glass doors. He wore a black polo shirt and khaki shorts, and was smiling, a bad sign, unless...

She rushed outside. "You found the moonstones?"

"No. Let's go to India together where you can pick out new gems yourself."

Where had last night's disappointment gone? She couldn't trust him. "I thought you said we have to postpone it. No, wait, cancel it. You were upset with me last night. I'm upset with me. I can't marry you in jail--" *Can't I ever say anything right the first time?*

"That's the thing. I can't let them arrest you, and I can't give up the way we make the boat rock and that cute way you talk in your sleep--"

"I talk in my sleep?" Her heartbeat flip-flopped in betrayal, like that fish her grandmother talked about. "Was I coherent? On the first try?"

"Very." His dimple slithered into place. A brow arched.

Her body went hot as the croissants probably burning now in her oven. "Jonathon, don't you see what's going on? You're in love with a dream person, not the real me."

Throwing his arms wide to embrace the lawn and gardens, he said. "Let's get married right here, right where you'll build your glass conservatory with birds and tropical plants blooming year-round despite the snow. Crystal Hagan could bring her goats and reindeer and alpaca so kids could have fun with a petting zoo. We'll make it a grand party. It won't be just for us. We'll share our happiness."

"Stop it. There you go again. You never listen to me." Every person in the restaurant waved at them. "Please leave. I'm busy."

She led him around the mansion to the parking lot, discovering her car was gone. Grandma Tracy must have seen him and sneaked away to do the deed. Alone. With no ally or alibi.

Kirsten backpedaled, grabbing his arm. "Why don't you stay and taste my new tomato bisque recipe?"

Jonathon beamed at her touch. "No, you're right. I'm interrupting. I'm going out to the yacht right now to start Tony fixing us something special for tonight. We'll plan our trip."

"No!" She launched into his arms and kissed him soundly. "No. Stay. Stay here and help me in the kitchen. I'm swamped." *I'm drowning in lies. Goodness but he smells good, like sunshine.*

While Jonathon sliced tomatoes into wedges, she hurried outside to check for the car. Nothing.

Another hour went by. Jonathon graduated to waiter. There was no sign of her grandmother. She called home but got no answer.

Then the deputy showed up at the hostess stand. She hoped he only wanted lunch.

"I have a wonderful dandelion medley salad today tossed with dressing made with a local strawberry wine."

Taking off his hat, the officer smiled. "Sounds lovely, ma'am, but I'm here for Mr. VanBrocklin. We caught his thief."

Kirsten's body turned to stone.

Jonathon hustled up beside her. "Who was it? Bored teenagers?"

The officer said, "No, some blonde in red who says she can't remember her name. I've had to crack down on the blonde jokes at the station."

"But she handed over the moonstones? They're precious to us." He winked at Kirsten.

"Not yet," the officer said, "but a night in jail usually loosens up their tongues."

Kirsten excused herself to the kitchen, where she sank into despair. Not only was she headed for jail, but more important--she'd betrayed Jonathon. By mentioning the moonstones to her grandmother, Kirsten had set up the heist. The Peplinskis had to leave Moonstone. Now.

With lightning bugs sparking in the night air, Kirsten pulled into the driveway after work to find the garage door open and the light on. Her mother was hammering on a birdhouse roof.

"Mom? Shouldn't you be in bed by now?"

It was after ten. Her mother had taken over the garage with a six-foot folding table and birdhouse parts in stacks everywhere. "A martin house."

They sold well because martins ate mosquitoes. Kirsten slapped at one biting her arm. "I have something to tell you about grandma."

"I heard. Tell me, what do you think of the shape of this house?"

It broke Kirsten's heart to think about uprooting her mother from this. The house had little pillars, a White House effect. "Snazzy."

"I built two of them tonight. A couple from Minneapolis told me they'd stop back for one tomorrow."

Kirsten's heart lurched. So they weren't going to discuss grandma and the stolen gems. She pulled a rickety chair over, twisting it around so she could lean her chin on the back. "Why did you want to come back to Moonstone? Really?"

"I was born here."

"I know that. But after everything we did...?"

"Are you embarrassed by me and Grandma?"

Kirsten hesitated too long and her mother added, "I don't mind being the crazy lady who makes birdhouses. My blood pressure's better than it ever was."

Kirsten was sure hers had skyrocketed. She handed her mother a pine cone. "Have you heard about me screwing up everything possible?"

Ellen applied glue to the pine cone. "This must be about a man. I saw all the bikinis, including yours. The only reason women strip is because of men."

"Why did I do that? Stupidly I fell right back into our old habits."

With an artist's brush, Ellen painted the pine cone green. "When you rely on instincts instead of facing the truth, bad things happen. Didn't the judge tell us that? The truth is what will get you out of this. Tell the man the truth. Grow up, dear. Being an adult means telling the truth. Your father never got that. He never told me the truth. Love is about telling the truth."

"Love? Why does everybody around me assume I'm in love?"

"Honey, I didn't say that. He thinks he's in love with you. And you're not sure. So quit this silly war you have and instead test him."

"Test? How?"

"Truth is the test of a relationship. Tell him the absolute truth of who you are and see how he reacts. He'll either walk away, or he'll stay because he needs you."

Kirsten was more confused than ever. How could Jonathon possibly need her? "So what do I do?"

"I don't know, honey. Your grandma and I led you down the wrong path. It's time you broke our pattern. This family needs a new leader. I trust you. So do the women of Moonstone."

Leader? Trust? Margie had hugged her and said they were friends. But why? She rushed in the house and called Rita Johnson. "Why did all of you go along with my risqué plan so easily?"

Rita laughed. "We didn't. We're scared out of minds wearing those thongs and push-up bras. But that's why it worked. We needed to be shaken out of our dull lives. Some of us hadn't worn a bathing suit since high school. Isn't that sad? Missing the summer breeze on your skin? We came out of hiding because of you. Thank goodness you don't hide from anything. We needed you to stand up to Jonathon VanBrocklin."

Kirsten swallowed. She'd done all that for them? They thought she was brave? That she didn't hide? She'd been hiding for much of her life. Had these women somehow pulled her out into the sunlight and breeze, too? She felt like a fledgling ready to fly for the first time.

But why did Jonathon need her? She got back in her car.

To Kirsten's surprise, several cars were parked at the dock in Port Cliff. A party seemed in progress on the yacht. Light from the windows wobbled across the dark pier.

After taking off her flip-flops, she sneaked on, padding to the shadows near the cabin door.

Several men were inside. One of them said, "You have to stop this topless business. If you don't, my wife is going to continue parading about town, and frankly, I don't want to share her. She's damn sexy. A man can't handle other men looking that way at his woman."

Another grumbled, "I can't even go to work because I can't get out of bed. I'd forgotten my wife was that sexy. My johnny's happy, but I'm tired."

Kirsten smiled.

Yet another deep voice said, "The women want the boat gone, and by golly, I like the way my wife's been thinking lately. I gotta do right by her."

As the men marched out, Kirsten slunk into the shadows. She waited until the last car left the dock, then taking a deep breath, she came out of hiding. "So what're you going to do? Keep your business, or keep their marriages intact?"

Jonathon whipped around, lacking his usual smile. "I didn't realize I had the power to save marriages." He turned to lean on the railing. This was a new Jonathon.

Joining him, she peered up at the stars. "So, things got serious on you in a way you never expected. Why did you bring the topless boat here?"

"I work with Peter LeBarron. The boat was his idea."

Kirsten flinched, the breeze chilling her bare arms. So he worked with her very own boss. When in town, Peter lived upstairs in the North Pole mansion with his father, Henri LeBarron. "Was I part of a dare?"

He edged closer, a thumb frisking with her chin, making the starlight in his blue eyes change to stormy electricity. "No. I wanted you. I was growling about all the women I dated who seemed to just want me for my money when Peter told me about Moonstone and the new business you'd started, how you were taking a risk, starting with no money and loving it. He had a newspaper clipping from your opening. I liked the way you looked in your apron and hat. I could tell you worked a lot harder to earn a buck than I ever did. There was something pure about you that I needed."

That jolted her. That was what he needed from her? Her purity? Her soul felt like an Etch-A-Sketch just shaken. "You fell for an image, Jonathon. I'm a lie. You forgot to ask about the true me."

"I'm sorry--"

"No, it's my fault. I didn't ask much about you either. We both assumed things. Maybe we were both too chicken to tell the truth because we enjoyed the moment, as they say." Her heartbeat banged against her chest wall. Could she take this next step? Could she lose him? How fast? "Let me show you who I really am."

In minutes Kirsten was driving down a winding gravel road into blackness. She stopped the car in a weedy parking lot, then got out with flashlight in hand to lead him toward the decrepit building in front of them.

Jonathon asked, "An old supper club?"

"This is where I grew up. Grandma Tracy bought it maybe twenty years ago. We lived upstairs." Her hand went sweaty around the flashlight. "This is where I learned how to lie. It's how I ended up in front of a judge facing a jail term."

His lack of response hit her like a poison arrow. Slow death was underway.

Inside, Kirsten's light beam revealed beer cans and liquor bottles from clandestine parties. In her memory, she heard men's bawdy guffaws, smelled the heavy, blue cigar smoke.

"This is where my grandmother ran a little business, especially popular during deer hunting season. The place featured a special kind of 'dears', including my grandmother."

Behind her, Jonathon cleared his throat. "So my topless touring boat was not so funny to you."

"Oh, none of us worked as prostitutes, but I saw women go out the door with men. My grandmother did her share of pole dancing. At six or seven years old, I remember how people looked at me in town and how mothers would veer their kids away from me."

"I'm sorry I said those things about not having friends."

"You actually woke me up. I hadn't realized how much I'd gone into a shell to avoid the past hurt. But there's something even deeper I have to tell you. It goes beyond my embarrassment or the way we were shunned."

The air stirred and she sensed Jonathon was going to put an arm around her. She stepped away, not wanting to fall prey to the way his protective arms made her melt.

"We had money that lasted from deer season in November through the holidays just fine. But the rest of the year got meager. My grandmother resorted to her own brand of shopping. She convinced me that if we couldn't afford things and we really needed them, it was okay to borrow them. She always said we'd pay for them later."

"And later never came." He shifted in the dark.

She bounced the light beam into every corner, rooting out the past. "She'd distract the clerks and I'd stuff my pockets with everything from food to jewelry."

She wandered toward the low stage. "I never liked being poor. You see, Jonathon--" She choked up. "You see how silly it is to think I'd marry you. That would be the biggest con of all time. Grandma even drifted into her old ways this week. She wants me to marry you so we're all filthy rich. I'm no different than any of those other women you dated."

Jonathon shifted his weight, his dark look killing her inside.

She went on. "When Grandma sensed the heat was about to come down, we headed for Chicago to start a new life. But Grandma couldn't break her habit. The shoes of mine you have? She stole those--I just found out, by the way--the day before she entered prison for a year. She lied and took all the blame herself so that mom and I got off. The judge saw that I had changed.

He sentenced me to finish college while Grandma cleaned toilets in a women's prison."

She paused to steady her breathing. "The trauma gave my mother a heart attack. She almost died because of me. Jonathon, you'd be a laughingstock for hooking up with the Peplinski con artists."

"But wouldn't it be an adventure?"

It was an empty attempt at a joke. "Since I was a little girl what I really wanted to be was normal. I dreamed of having a real job, of making it on my own, becoming rich the old-fashioned way. Yes, I dreamed of being filthy rich. Jonathon, I don't think I could get over the feeling of using you, even if I loved you, too. My love wouldn't be pure. And that's the truth."

Jonathon looked into her eyes long and hard, sending a tremor to her soul. Something had shifted within him and between them.

Neither talked during the drive back.

From her car, she watched Jonathon climb the ladder, then disappear inside the cabin.

The boat shifted from the dock, its engine rumbling, stirring the brackish water.

Kirsten watched until Jonathon's yacht became a speck in the darkness, slipping away into the vastness of Lake Superior. That was when she finally cried buckets, because she'd just gotten what she'd wanted all along. She'd gotten rid of the guy who owned the tart ship.

Chapter 7

The next day Kirsten prepared the salad bar at The Jingle Bell Inn like a robot. Her heart wasn't in anything that wouldn't last. Except her freedom.

Earlier, she'd driven to Superior to pick up her grandmother. "Just like that, they let you go?"

"Honey, I don't have the moonstones on me. They didn't mess up the house too much this morning, did they?"

Two detectives had knocked on their door at six a.m. with a search warrant. "No, one of them even swept the kitchen floor because he'd tracked in gravel."

"That's so nice."

"Grandma, what the hell did you do with the moonstones?"

"There are other women who had plenty of access to that boat."

"The tarts?"

"No, dear. Who might *you* have told about the gems besides me and your mother?"

Groaning, she admitted, "Every woman in Moonstone because of my big mouth."

When the restaurant filled with women eating lunch, Kirsten counted her suspects. Tootsie knew about her past and might want to run her out of town. Lily loved her pearls; could she also love that other white gem? What about Margie, desperate for grocery store success? Maybe Rita's husband wanted to expand the hardware store. Maybe Jeri? She made pennies driving the bus.

As the plates emptied, Kirsten noticed a silence in the room. Her heart sank.

Lily got up. "The men are missing again. What're we going to do about it?"

In her self-pity, Kirsten hadn't noticed that no men sat in the restaurant. Had Jonathon started up a new fishing tour with pole dancing because she'd opened her big mouth about it?

Misery drizzled down Kirsten's spine like over-cooked gravy. "I guess my plan backfired."

"No, your plan worked," Rita said. "Nobody really watches the late shows anymore because we're busy doing you-know-what."

With prim smiles, the women elbowed each other.

Kirsten wrung her apron. "I don't understand. You all looked mad at me a moment ago. Some of you still do."

Tootsie said, "Because we need a new plan from you to get the men back."

Lily said, "You did more in three days for Moonstone than Bob ever did as mayor. Sorry, Tootsie."

Tootsie tossed it off with a hand. "The old coot needed to retire from the stress long ago. I propose we make Kirsten Peplinski our new, permanent mayor."

Kirsten yelped, "You can't do that."

"Why not?" Crystal asked.

Kirsten looked at all the imploring faces. They deserved the truth. "I'm sorry, but I have to quit."

"Quit?!" The women gasped as one.

Margie, her bosom threatening the buttons of a skimpy, sexy, lemon-colored blouse, said, "We need your ideas and your restaurant. People are coming to my IGA looking for exotic ingredients so they can duplicate your dishes."

"They are? I'm exotic?"

"I'm finally selling more than milk and tampons."

Crystal rushed up to Kirsten. "For my bridal shower, you have to make your Xango again for dessert. Nobody here had ever heard of Xango until you came to town."

The women broke into a chant with "Xango". The unexpected outpouring of friendship overwhelmed Kirsten. Guilt over not being more forthcoming took hold. She sputtered out the saga of the Peplinski women.

Kirsten took off her apron. "I can't embarrass you. That's why I have to leave Moonstone."

Lily stood up again. "So you never pole danced yourself?"

"No," Kirsten said.

Jeri said, "I've heard it's good exercise."

Several heads bobbed. Tootsie said, "They have classes over there in Duluth. Didn't you see that place next to where we bought lingerie?"

Lily took off her pearls and twirled them. "Maybe your grandmother could teach us so we wouldn't have to drive to Duluth."

Just like that, they forgave the Peplinski women. Kirsten felt terrible telling them, "I'm not sure of where the men are. And I told Jonathon I couldn't marry him."

The women flashed stony looks.

Tootsie said, "Well, honey, you better get him back."

"Why?"

"He has our men," snapped Rita. "It has to be him. Maybe he's found a new dock to call home. You get your glow back and in the meantime we'll learn pole dancing to dazzle the male of the species. You taught us to fight for love and, by golly, we're gonna fight, right, ladies?"

Kirsten groaned while the women hurried out. They saw a future in all this; she knew Jonathon was gone.

Then, there he was, standing outside the sliding glass door with nothing on!

"Oh my--" She raced forward, grabbing a tablecloth. Unlocking the door, she thrust it at him. "What are you doing?"

"I'm here for lunch."

"You *are* a lunatic."

"I love how you say that." Letting the tablecloth drop, he walked toward the kitchen. "What should we fix?"

"You better fix this latest problem of yours." She stopped, fired up for a fight, though being mooned by him edged her toward a smile. "You can't be running that boat again. I heard what the men said. They want it gone. I thought you were gone. I won."

"And how does winning feel?"

Darn him. She kept her loser feelings to herself.

He found her folded chef's apron and pulled it on over his head. "I sold that boat early this morning to Bob Winters."

"Tootsie's husband?" That made no sense.

"Here, tie this for me. Please." He turned around, showing his bare bum.

Heat coursing through her, she tied the apron strings. Then she smacked his butt.

"Hey!" he said, turning around.

"You deserved that. What's going on?" He shouldn't be here; she shouldn't be feeling this geyser of joy inside herself. "Why are you here?"

"Did you realize that there are only two places where we've had fun? Where we get along? Where you listen to me? The bedroom and the kitchen. I want to talk. We could find a motel or--"

"The kitchen's fine." Her skin flushed hot.

In her kitchen he grabbed a pan. "Last night I took you at your word. You didn't want to marry me. I headed back to the Duluth harbor, ready to dry-dock the boat when I started feeling like an even bigger fool for believing you. Where's the butter?"

She pointed to a cupboard. "I didn't lie."

"You said you couldn't marry me, which really meant you couldn't marry me under the circumstances I'd set up. So I made a call or two, got the word out early this morning that I needed men who were willing to test the finest fishing craft on Lake Superior with professional fishing guides. And I was looking to hire several guides."

Kirsten relaxed, but only a little. She was facing a bare butt, after all. "So they're fishing for real this time. But I'm not letting you charm me into whatever it is you're trying to do with your nudity and warm butter."

"As long as my naughty bits don't end up in the butter, we'll be fine."

Hot all over, she turned off the flame and blocked him from her stove. "We can't just pick up where we left off."

"Why not?"

"Because I'm your thief. I blabbed about the moonstones and gave somebody in town an open invitation to steal them. And it would always be this way. I bumble through life."

"Bumble? I guess I have to stay so you don't hurt yourself while bumbling. And I have to stay until we find the moonstones."

Kirsten's heart skittered about. She picked up a spatula and shook it at him. "Get out of here."

"Or what? You'll spank me?" He flashed a dimply grin. "That confirms it--I need you in my life."

Her heart skipped a beat. She lowered the spatula. "Why do you need me? Really?"

"I need the way you create havoc in my heart, and the way you make me dance in the kitchen." He danced around, gyrating, wiggling his butt, then he came at her with a gleam in his eyes...as he glided past her and out the door.

Jonathon marched out to the street, then down the sidewalk in only the apron.

"Jonathon?" She trotted after him waving the spatula. "What are you doing?"

He kept trotting down the street, then shouted at cars driving by, "I want Peppy to marry me. What do you think, folks?"

Kirsten wanted to melt away.

Cars honked. Tourists gave Jonathon a thumbs up.

Jonathon raced on past the post office, the apron flashing his bare butt. Kirsten called out, "Where are you going?"

"To see if I can find twelve women who'll say they're your friends. I want twelve reasons for you to stop hiding from life, twelve reasons to stop being afraid of me because you're embarrassed that you're not as good as me or anybody else because of your past. Or, do I have it wrong? Are you too good for love at first sight? Do you believe I'm a liar?"

Drat. She stopped. The whole town paused, too. Everybody stared at her from their cars, the park swings, the bait shop down on the corner.

Then Rita waved from the post office. Then women all over Moonstone clapped for her. Her heart swelled. But fear crept back in. She didn't deserve this happiness. It was a bad trick, like her father leaving her forever. She needed to talk with her mother. Ellen Peplinski would set her daughter straight.

As she ran over to the table in the park, sunlight glinted off something shiny, almost blinding her. *Oh no!*

"Mother? How could you?"

Ellen smiled. "Shhh. I had to do something or your grandmother would still be in jail."

Along with the barrettes, buttons, and bows glued on the birdhouses were moonstones. "These were sitting in the kitchen this morning."

"The detectives didn't give them a glance."

So her grandmother had stolen the jewels, and her mother had saved her grandmother by hiding them in plain sight. Did the two women do this to get Kirsten and Jonathon together? Kirsten didn't have time to pursue it. A ruckus over at the IGA caught their attention and Ellen said, "Honey, how long are you going to torture that man? If only your father had shown me that much love..."

Kirsten's heartbeat raced at the sight of Jonathon beginning to climb a lamp post. She raced to catch up to him. "Get down. I have something to tell you."

Margie came flouncing out, hugging them both. "Antonio just proposed. In front of all my customers."

"Antonio?" Then Kirsten and Jonathon both echoed, "Tony?!"

The skinny chef wandered out of the store, looking sheepish, but after his face got buried in the breasts of his fiancée's hug, he went all smiles.

Kirsten took Jonathon by the arm. "I have something important to tell you."

"You'll marry me?"

She looked about. The women of Moonstone were holding their hands at the ready, waiting to clap for her. "Yes," she said, leaping into his arms, "but first I need you to buy a dozen birdhouses."

Four weeks later that August, the tables at The Jingle Bell Inn were festooned with birdhouse centerpieces made by Ellen Peplinski, though the rooftops had been relieved of precious gems.

Kirsten went teary-eyed at the twelve friends wearing moonstones and Tiffany blue dresses who lined the patio where the conservatory would soon be built.

She messed up her vows totally and forgot Jonathon's name, but having twelve bridesmaids helped. In unison they chorused, "I, Kirsten, take you, Jonathon."

Jonathon kissed her in a way that put even more spark in her eyes.

Much later, under starlight, Jonathon carried his bride down the sweeping lawn to a new pier. Tootsie and Bob Winters had rechristened Jonathon's boat the "The Honeymoon Suite". Mr. and Mrs. VanBrocklin were their first customers.

Kirsten gazed into her husband's eyes. The moon, smiling, rested on his shoulder.

"What're you thinking?" he asked, nuzzling her neck in a prelude.

"I'm thinking that I never got my five-hundred-dollar shoes back from you."

"Didn't you notice what your grandmother was wearing under her bridesmaid gown?"

Kirsten groaned. "She's going to be a problem, you know."

"Not if we give her something to occupy her time. Like great-grandchildren."

To Kirsten's delight, Jonathon kissed her until the moon blushed, then he took her aboard for a cruise among the stars on the big fluffy bed.

If you enjoyed this author's book, then please place a review up at the site of purchase, and any social media sites you frequent!

You can find ALL our books on our website at:

http://www.writers-exchange.com

All our romances:

http://www.writers-exchange.com/category/genres/romance/

All Christine's Books:

http://www.writers-exchange.com/christine-desmet/

About the Author

Christine **DeSmet** is an award-winning fiction writer and professional screenwriter. She is the author of the bestselling *Fudge Shop Mystery Series* and the popular novella series called *Mischief in Moonstone*.

She is a Distinguished Faculty Associate in Writing at University of Wisconsin-Madison where she teaches novel writing and screenwriting and directs the annual summer Write-by-the-Lake Writer's Workshop & Retreat. Through her master classes she has seen many of her adult students become published.

She is also a professional writing coach in the UW-Madison Writers' Institute conference's Pathway to Publication program.

Christine is a member of Mystery Writers of America, Sisters in Crime, Wisconsin Writers Association, Wisconsin Screenwriters Association, and other professional associations.

Christine is active on Facebook and you can also find her at http://www.ChristineDeSmet.com

Christine's author page at Writers Exchange E-Publishing is: http://www.writers-exchange.com/christine-desmet/

If you want to read more about books by this author, they are listed on the following pages...

Fudge Shop Mystery Series

Deadly Fudge Divas

A taste of trouble is in the air when a group of well-heeled, fudge-loving women descend on Ava Oosterling's newly acquired and lovingly refurbished bed & breakfast inn for a chocolate lovers' getaway.

When one of the women turns up dead--and Ava's grandfather is a prime suspect--Ava plunges into the thick of a murder case stickier than her candy store's line of Fairy Tale fudge flavors and the chocolate facials the women adore at the local spa.

It's springtime and the start of the tourist season in Fishers' Harbor, Wisconsin. Ava has opened the Blue Heron Inn with the help of handsome construction worker Dillon Rivers. Unfortunately, Dillon's mother--Ava's ex-mother-in-law--is among the secretive divas who become suspects along with Grandpa.

Ava turns for help from her friends but they have troubles, too. One is eager for a wedding proposal to unfold on live television, while another friend is expecting her first baby and asks Ava to assist with the birth.

Everything and everybody Ava loves seems in chaos--her fudge shop, her inn, her family, and her own friendships... Until she uncovers a thirty-year-old secret of the "deadly fudge divas".

Publisher: https://www.writers-exchange.com/deadly-fudge-divas/

Undercover Fudge

Candy shop owner Ava Oosterling has her hands full when her best friend Pauline Mertens takes a summer job as a wedding coordinator--with the nuptials and reception scheduled in mere days in the back yard of Ava's Blue Heron Inn overlooking Lake Michigan's bay.

To help out her best friend, Ava is intent on making the table favors-- edible fudge lighthouses patterned after their county's 11 lighthouses.

Unfortunately, trying to finish the luscious ruby chocolate lighthouses becomes elusive. The sheriff informs Ava that a band of thieves storming the country may have targeted this wedding. And that's because there's proof Pauline's mother is associated with the thieves.

When the sheriff asks Ava to go undercover, she finds herself in an emotional quagmire. Pauline's mother only recently returned to Fishers' Harbor after years of estrangement from her daughter. And, Coletta Mertens now works as the housekeeper at Ava's inn. Has Ava's fudge-and-wine hospitality provided a hideout for a criminal?

Unfortunately, "until death do us part" takes a murderous twist involving Ava's Grandpa Gil, the dog Lucky Harbor, and Ava's own beau.

Publisher: https://www.writers-exchange.com/undercover-fudge/

Holly Jolly Fudge Folly

An early, deep snow has gifted Fishers' Harbor, Wisconsin, with a perfect setting for the holiday celebration. Unfortunately removing snow from Main Street for the parade reveals the dead tax assessor with a knife in him-- containing Grandpa Gil's fingerprints.

It's clearly a setup and one that keeps Ava and Grandpa Gil under the watchful eyes of Sheriff Tollefson. Who wants Grandpa to miss playing Santa Claus in the Christmas parade and why? Who's being naughty instead of nice?

Grandpa doesn't help his case with talk of leaving town for good--words that chill Ava worse than the weather. She can't imagine life without Grandpa's warm hugs and laughter.

When vandals strike the historic shop and someone leaves Ava and fiancé Dillon Rivers for dead in the snow, Ava wonders if she may need the magical help of Santa's elves to solve the holiday folly.

Publisher: https://www.writers-exchange.com/holly-jolly-fudge-folly/

Mischief in Moonstone Series

Nestled against the sparkling shores of Lake Superior, the tiny village of Moonstone is anything but ordinary. Between romantic entanglements, quirky neighbors, and mysteries that seem to pop up with every season, the locals know life here comes with a generous dose of laughter and surprise. From silkie chickens and a giant prehistoric beaver skeleton to kidnapped reindeer and holiday hijinks, mischief is always waiting just around the corner. Fall in love with the humorous, heartwarming adventures of Moonstone--where romance meets mayhem in the most delightful ways.

Novella 1: When Rudolf was Kidnapped

Crystal Hagan's first-graders are in panic mode. Their beloved holiday reindeer, Rudolph, has been stolen from the school's live Christmas display. Without him, the children are convinced Christmas is canceled.

The trail of mischief leads to Peter LeBarron, the wealthy recluse who lives in a mansion locals call the "North Pole." To Crystal's shock, Peter freely admits to taking Rudolph--but he refuses to give him back without some romantic negotiations of his own.

With the holiday countdown ticking, Crystal must juggle her students' worries, a stolen reindeer, and an unexpected suitor who may have just stolen her heart.

Humorous, heartwarming, and filled with small-town Christmas magic, this novella is perfect for fans of cozy romance and holiday cheer.

Publisher: https://www.writers-exchange.com/when-rudolph-was-kidnapped/

Novella 2: Misbehavin' in Moonstone

Kirsten Peplinski has worked hard to open her dream restaurant on the shores of Lake Superior. But when the men of Moonstone start disappearing in the evenings--and her business suffers--she discovers the shocking reason: a touring boat offering topless entertainment just outside town limits.

Determined to put an end to the mischief, Kirsten confronts the boat's infuriatingly handsome owner, Jonathon VanBrocklin. Instead of backing down, Jonathon kidnaps her--claiming undressing and marriage are the only items on his menu.

Caught between outrage and unexpected attraction, Kirsten faces the wildest adventure of her life. Will she escape this reckless scheme, or discover that true love sometimes arrives in the most mischievous packages?

Humorous, romantic, and funny, cheeky, and charming, *Misbehavin' in Moonstone* is a sizzling small-town escape.

Publisher: https://www.writers-exchange.com/misbehavin-in-moonstone/

Novella 3: Mrs. Claus and the Moonstone Murder

New county deputy Lily Schuster is still learning the ropes when trouble strikes in Moonstone, Wisconsin. On her second day, she arrests archaeologist Marcus Linden for trespassing--only to find herself turning to him for help when a pie contest judge ends up murdered.

The suspects? None other than Henri LeBarron, the town's beloved eighty-four-year-old Santa, and his scandalous new companion, the alluring Felicity Starr. Both women are vying to become "Mrs. Claus" for the upcoming winter celebration--and their rivalry has turned deadly.

With August heat bearing down and tempers flaring, Lily must solve the case, keep her wits about her, and decide if Marcus's kisses are worth more than his alibis.

Quirky, romantic, and full of small-town mischief, *Mrs. Claus and the Moonstone Murder* blends mystery with a heart-stealing romance.

Publisher: https://www.writers-exchange.com/mrs-claus-and-the-moonstone-murder/

Novella 4: When the Dead People Brought a Dish-to-Pass

Three days before Halloween, Alyssa Swain finds a dead man in his car. But when she returns with help, the body has vanished.

Things only get stranger when the supposed corpse--scruffy, tall John Christopherson--appears on her doorstep very much alive...or at least claiming to be. John insists she summoned him to help prepare for a Halloween party, and he refuses to leave her house--or her heart.

But midnight on Halloween looms, and Alyssa must find a way to keep John from crossing into the afterlife forever.

Funny, eerie, and tender, When the Dead People Brought a Dish-to-Pass is a paranormal romance that blends small-town charm with Halloween magic.

Publisher: https://www.writers-exchange.com/when-the-dead-people-brought-a-dish-to-pass/

Novella 5: A Moonstone Wedding

Margie Mueller thought wedding jitters were normal--until her fiancé sent her a fertility rug.

She's no spring chicken, and the idea of raising a brood of Farina babies makes her panic. But before she can call the whole thing off, Tony's boisterous family descends on Moonstone with their parties, opinions, and endless interference.

Then a dead man turns up--wrapped in that same fertility rug. Suddenly, Margie's wedding isn't just in danger of collapsing under family chaos--it's at the center of a murder mystery. And Tony may know more than he's admitting.

Funny, quirky, and laced with small-town mischief, A Moonstone Wedding is a romantic novella with a deadly twist.

Publisher: https://www.writers-exchange.com/a-moonstone-wedding/

Novella 6: The Moonstone Fire

John "Bozeman" Hall has seen it all--longhorn cattle, grizzly hunts, even rattlesnake suppers. But nothing prepares him for Moonstone, Wisconsin.

When a suspicious fire destroys the newlyweds Crystal and Peter LeBarron's farm cabin, Bozeman is determined to track down the arsonist. His first suspect? A young homeless mother and her son, squatting in a cave on the property.

But the closer he gets to the truth, the more Bozeman discovers that danger isn't the only spark in town--so is the pull of unexpected love.

The Moonstone Fire delivers a sizzling blend of small-town mystery, heartwarming romance, and the quirky mischief Moonstone is known for.

Publisher: https://www.writers-exchange.com/the-moonstone-fire/

Coming November 2025...

Novella 7: All She Wore Was a Bow

Kincaid Hunter, professional bull rider and decorated veteran, has never been tamed--least of all by the thought of marriage. But when a good friend back home in Wisconsin plans a Christmas wedding, Kincaid can't resist riding in to try and stop him from making what he thinks is a big mistake.

What Kincaid doesn't expect is to be lassoed himself--by a wedding planner dressed as Mrs. Claus, with a sparkle in her eyes and a bow for every occasion.

Soon, the cowboy who vowed he'd never walk down the aisle discovers that love can tie a knot tighter than any rope.

All She Wore Was a Bow is a festive small-town romance full of humor, heart, and holiday magic.

Publisher: https://www.writers-exchange.com/the-moonstone-fire/

Coming Soon:

Novella 8: Pest Control

Novella 9: The Big Love & Murder Shilly-Shally in Moonstone

You can find ALL our books up on our website at:

http://www.writers-exchange.com

All our romances:

http://www.writers-exchange.com/category/genres/romance/

All Christine's Books:

http://www.writers-exchange.com/christine-desmet/